The Adve  ...angers

Book 1   Ballcourt of Death

What was it like to sail on a pirate ship? Would it be fun to run away with the circus? What were bathrooms like a hundred years ago? What is the inside of a tomb like? Who built the Sphinx? What is the best way to eat candy? What is it like to be thrown out of a boat into freezing water in the middle of a blizzard, without a hat? Is it possible to meet someone for the second time in ten years before you meet them the first time? When the time comes, will you be brave enough to save someone's life?

The Strangers, six children thrown together by fate and a love of oatmeal cookies, have asked all these questions and more. Many more. Strange House lets them find the answers to all these questions the hard way. In person.

The Strangers series will take you on adventures to exciting places and times. Thoroughly researched and historically accurate, the tales will unfold the lives and times of people from various points in the world's history.

BALLCOURT OF DEATH
by
John Buja

Illustrated by Melody Morrison

Text copyright© 2000 by John Buja
Illustrations copyright© 2000 by Melody Morrison
All rights reserved
Raven Rock Publishing
21 Burwash Dr.
Yellowknife NT X1A 2V1 Canada

Canadian Cataloguing in Publication Data

Buja, John E. (John Edwin), 1957-
    Ballcourt of death

(The adventures of the strangers ; 1)
ISBN 1-894303-23-7

    1. Mayas – Juvenile fiction. I. Morrison, Melody, 1971 – II.
Title. III. Series: Buja, John E. (John Edwin), 1957-
Adventures of the strangers ; 1.
PS8553.U456B34 2000   jC813'.6   C00-910629-4
PZ7.B911135Ba 2000

Printed in Canada by Artisan Press Ltd.
Yellowknife, Northwest Territories.

Dedication

For my mother, Vera Buja, who instilled in me a love of reading and history. I can never thank you enough.

Acknowledgements

This could not have been finished without the help, support, and encouragement of my wife Dianne, the real Miss Kane.

The children of Dianne's grade five and six classes over the years inspired many of the characters in this book. Thanks to you all for being who you are.

I'd like to extend a special thanks to Roya Shaji, for reading the manuscript and giving me that reader's perspective I needed the most.

CHAPTER ONE

"Run! Run! RUN! No! No, the other way! Yes! Yes! YES! Goal!"

Curly red hair swatted everyone around her as Prunella leapt for joy. She waved her head back and forth, a smile as wide as a mile across her face.

"If you hit me with your hair one more time," said Ketiwe with a little annoyance, "I'll cut it all off. Prue," she added.

Prunella glared at her friend. "Prue rhymes with poo and that won't do." Ketiwe stared back, her face impassive. "I'm telling you, I may just sue. Keep calling me Prue, you'll be black and blue," she bellowed. Her face was almost as red as her hair. "Got it?"

"Calm down, Prunella," said Ketiwe calmly. "I had to get your attention. You get too excited. It's just a name."

"Then get it right."

"Sure. At least I can breathe again without hair in my face."

Prunella said nothing. The crowd at the edge of the soccer field began to cheer. Prunella began to jump around again. "Did you see what Jozef did? Did you?"

Ketiwe nodded towards the soccer field. "Here he comes now."

The Tyndale Falcons soccer team had just won the city championship, and Jozef Krypinski was the star of the team. He had scored three goals during the game, but the last, the game winner, had been the most spectacular. Jozef had moved the ball from his team's end of the field to the other end and the ball never once touched the ground. He had bounced it off his head, shoulders, knees, and feet. The ball had sailed over the heads of opposing players and straight into their net.

As Jozef approached the group of children waiting at the

side of the soccer field, Prunella said, "Now that's using your head. Magic."

Everyone was slapping Jozef on the back, proud of their star. Jozef smiled then blushed as Prunella hugged him. "Thank you, Nell. Your jokes get worse every day."

Ketiwe shook her head. She couldn't get over how Prunella liked to hug people. It didn't seem natural to be so huggy. There must be something weird in the water back in England where Prunella used to live. Ketiwe moved forward to congratulate Jozef, but backed away when she saw how muddy his uniform was. Instead, she patted him on the shoulder, then stared at her hand for a moment, making sure there was no dirt there.

"We're going to my house for some adventure," said Prunella. "Do you want to come along, Jozef?"

"Thank you, but I think I need to get clean." Jozef flicked a glob of mud from his wrist, barely missing Ketiwe who let out a little shriek of distaste. "Maybe I'll see you later. And thank you for coming to watch us play."

Ketiwe moved closer to Jozef. "Jozef, can you show us that trick you do with the ball before we go? It's so cool."

The others cheered. They always liked to see someone with talent show off a bit, especially when they were having so much fun.

Jozef went over to the coach, who was carrying a large net bag full of balls, and asked for the bag. He carried it back to the group, emptied it, and lined up ten soccer balls. About fifty feet away stood an outdoor basketball hoop.

"Ready?" he asked the kids who had formed a half-circle around him. "Okay." He kicked each ball in quick succession. Eight of the ten sailed smoothly through the hoop. One bounced off the backboard. The other sailed over the backboard and disappeared onto the roof of the school. "I

need some practice," said Jozef, hands on hips and head tilted, as he examined the distance between himself and the hoop.

The crowd disbursed and Prunella and Ketiwe helped Jozef retrieve the balls. As Jozef was putting the balls back into the bag, the coach said, "That's another ball the janitor will have to recover. You know how afraid he is of heights."

"Sorry," said Jozef, blushing again.

Despite the frown on her face, everyone knew the coach was proud of her star player. She took the bag and went into the school.

Prunella and Ketiwe stood side by side and watched as Jozef walked towards the school. He turned and waved back.

When Jozef was out of sight, Prunella turned to Ketiwe and said, "Shall we find the others and get started?"

Ketiwe brought a soccer ball out from behind her back where she had been hiding it. Prunella's eyes lit up.

"I want to try the trick," said Ketiwe. She placed the ball on the ground, lined up her shot and kicked the ball. It smacked hard into the side of the school well below the net and zoomed back at her.

Prunella intercepted the ball and lined up her own shot. Both girls held their breath as it looked like Prunella's kick would send the ball onto the roof. At the last second, the ball dipped and bounced off the gutter.

"We should go," said Prunella.

"One more try," Ketiwe said quietly as she placed the ball on the ground. She stood for a few seconds sizing up the situation, then ran at the ball.

Ketiwe's kick was more powerful than she realised. The ball smashed into the backboard and ricochetted onto the roof of the portable classroom behind the girls.

There was the sound of a bounce.

"That'll be the ball hitting the roof. I think that crunch

might have been the vent pipe."

Another bounce.

Ketiwe nodded. "The other side of the portable, heading for the parking lot."

A bounce and a splat.

Prunella thought for a moment, then said, "The school bus?"

Ketiwe shook her head in disagreement. "No, the Principal's car. He has that plastic roof-rack. That was the splat."

The girls stopped and looked at each other.

"The Principal's car!" they shouted in unison.

Both girls turned and raced for the gate at the end of the soccer field. Ketiwe leapt over a couple of puddles and had to do some fancy acrobatics when Prunella sent a spray of mud flying in her direction. Both reached the gate free of goo.

Breathless, Prunella said, "Are we finished having fun? Can we act like adults?"

Ketiwe looked at her friend and shouted, "No, we're kids. Let's keep having fun!"

With that, they ran off screaming down the road towards Prunella's house and adventure.

CHAPTER TWO

"I don't understand you, Ro," said Denis. "You know she's the girl's wrestling champ. You like to put your life at risk like that? One day she's going to roll you into a little ball and give you to Jozef for soccer practice."

"If she hits me, does that mean she likes me?" asked Rohan. His left arm was up to the shoulder in a sewer grate and his face rested on the sidewalk.

"Give it up, you know she likes Jozef," Denis said from where he was sitting on the walk next to Rohan.

"I know. But..."

Denis got to his knees. "What? Have you found it?"

Rohan grunted. "I've got my fingers around it. Help me up."

Denis grabbed Rohan's right arm and began to pull his friend to his feet.

Quickly, Rohan shouted, "Stop helping me up!"

Denis let go and Rohan slid back to the sidewalk. He was crouched beside the grate now, just his hand through the hole in its centre.

"What's the problem?" asked Denis as he sat down again.

Rohan looked frustrated. "I've got your Swiss army knife in my hand, but my hand won't fit through the hole while I'm making a fist."

Denis whistled. "Wow, you've got the skinniest arms in school. Why are your hands so fat?" He leaned back as Rohan tried to swat his head. "Maybe if you open your hand a little?" he suggested.

"No good. I'll drop the knife again. I don't want to put my hand back in the muck at the bottom."

Getting on his knees, Denis slipped his fingers through the hole in the grate next to the one that had trapped Rohan's fist. He tried to reach Rohan's fist, and Rohan tried to reach Denis, but neither could move far enough.

Denis sat back with a jarring thump. He shook his head and said, "Nuts. My dad gave me that knife for Christmas. We have to get it back."

Rohan took a grip on the grate with his right hand and tried to lift it. The grate didn't move. He gave it a sudden yank. There was a slight whooshing noise from the back of Rohan, but the grate still didn't move.

Denis recoiled in horror. "Did you?"

Rohan smiled but said nothing.

Carefully, Denis waddled back to the grate. He sniffed the air a few times, wrinkled his nose, then grasped the grate. "Sewer gas," he muttered.

Together the boys tried to lift the grate. It moved slightly but fell back into place when both boys gave up at the same time.

"Oh, no," said Rohan.

"What now?"

Prunella and Ketiwe walked up to the two boys and stared down at them.

"Trying to get back into your house?" asked Prunella.

Rohan and Denis looked at each other then glared at Prunella. Denis then explained about how he dropped his Swiss army knife down the grate. Rohan had volunteered to retrieve it because his arms were so skinny. Now they were stuck.

When Prunella and Ketiwe finally stopped laughing, Ketiwe stepped forward and said, "Move."

Denis got up and stood beside Prunella. Rohan got to his knees but kept a steady grip on the knife.

Ketiwe knelt, gripped the grate, and lifted it out of its socket. Rohan was forced to roll over as Ketiwe leaned the grate on its side. Denis took the knife from Rohan's hand, and Rohan pulled his hand back through the hole. Ketiwe calmly replaced the grate.

Denis tried to shake the mud off his knife. Rohan passed him one of the many handkerchiefs he always carried and Denis began to clean his prize. "Thanks for the help," he said to everyone.

"Yeah, thanks, Ketiwe," said Rohan.

Rohan stuck his grimy left hand out to shake Ketiwe's hand. As he thrust his hand forward, globs of sewer muck went flying. Ketiwe shrieked and ducked. Twice in one day! This was just too much. She stomped away from the other three and began to check her clothes for mud. The look on her face told the others to leave her alone for a while.

Rohan wiped his hands on a handkerchief. "So, what's happening?" he asked Prunella.

"Ketiwe and I were going to my place for some adventure."

Prunella looked over at her friend who was now trying to see the back of her shirt. She was spinning around like a dog chasing its tail, but no one laughed. The wrath of Ketiwe was not a good thing to call forth.

"You guys are welcome to come along," Prunella said, looking at Rohan and Denis in turn. "That is, unless you have another sewer you want to explore."

Rohan brightened at the idea. He turned to Denis and said, "There is that one over on Amery. The one with the extra wide opening."

Denis let out a long breath. Rohan looked so sincere when he was being a goof. "It's a tough choice, but I think Strange House will be more fun than a sewer. Right, Rohan?"

Rohan, whose attention was focussed on Ketiwe, looked back and said, "Huh? Sure."

Prunella began to walk in the direction of her house. Ketiwe fell in step beside her and the boys followed a few paces behind.

"Come on you two. We haven't got all day," Prunella said impatiently when she noticed how far back the boys had fallen.

"Yes, boss," said Denis as he handed back Rohan's handkerchief. He carefully placed the Swiss army knife back in his knapsack. It would be safe there until he could return it to its place of pride on his dresser at home.

Prunella favoured the boys with a grunt when they caught up to her and Ketiwe. She twirled around, nearly swatting Ketiwe in the face with her hair, pointed towards Strange House, and said, "Head 'em up and move 'em out."

Rohan and Denis gave each other a knowing look. Prunella had been watching old television shows again on the magic box. They quickly fell into place not wanting to get Prunella angry with them again.

CHAPTER THREE

Julia pedalled hard as she tried to keep up with Selamawit. The bike wobbled a little because Julia held a stopwatch in her right hand. She wasn't used to riding bikes anyway, preferring roller blades, but her skates were in the shop being repaired. Selamawit suddenly turned right and Julia nearly went through the intersection. At the last second, she yanked on the handlebars and followed after her friend.

Selamawit put on a burst of speed as she saw her destination. The oak tree at the corner of the Strange estate hung over the stone fence that circled the estate. It was a convenient place to stop because Selamawit could also see Prunella and the rest of the gang a few yards beyond the tree.

Julia was puffing as she brought the bike up along side Selamawit. Selamawit's feet pounded on the road, her knees rising high with every stride. As she passed the oak, she looked over at Julia and smiled.

The button on the top of the stopwatch clicked and Julia said, "Five minutes and fifteen seconds."

Selamawit gently slowed herself and walked for a short while. She leaned over, hands on knees, and took some deep breaths. Sweat glistened on her forehead.

"That was a very good time. Thank you for your help, Julia," Selamawit said in her usual perfect English. She tried to learn as many languages as possible, and she was always careful to speak them correctly.

Julia remained quiet, as was her way, and simply acknowledged the thanks with a nod.

"Shall we join the others?" asked Selamawit and trotted off.

With a grimace of pain, Julia dismounted. She rubbed her sore backside and walked the bike after Selamawit. There had to be an easier way to help Selamawit train for the track team, she thought.

"Hello, everyone. What is happening?"

Ketiwe let out a yelp. "Selamawit! Must you creep up on us like that?"

"I am sorry. I walk quietly to keep out of trouble," said Selamawit. She looked down at her shoes then glanced up. "Is that mud on your shirt, Ketiwe?"

While Ketiwe tried to look at her back and find the mud that wasn't there, Prunella stepped over to Selamawit.

"We're going exploring. Do you want to come?"

"Will there be any cannibals this time? I did not like them very much. Their cooking pots were very uncomfortable."

"There better not be any cannibals," said Julia flatly. She stared at Prunella waiting for an answer.

Prunella ignored Julia. "We're not going anywhere near cannibals or anyone dangerous." She looked at the others. "You guys got any ideas?"

Rohan was teasing Ketiwe about the mud on her back. Whenever she tried to reach the spot, he would tell her it was somewhere else. Denis finally assured her there was nothing on her shirt.

When he heard Prunella's question, Denis spoke up. "I was reading about the Maya for a school project. They were very interesting and didn't eat people at all."

"That sounds like a good idea," Prunella replied. "Any objections?"

The others all nodded in agreement, except Rohan who was being held in an awkward headlock by Ketiwe.

"Let's go then," said Prunella.

Prunella led her friends to the main gates of Strange House. A six-foot wall ran around the grounds from either side of the wrought iron gates. At its top was a row of sharp iron spikes. The original builder of the house did not like trespassers.

"Okay," whispered Prunella, "we can't go in the front way. Uncle Archie might see us and figure out what we're doing. I think he's still mad about the last time and the cannibals."

"You don't think they were really going to eat us, do you?" asked Rohan from under Ketiwe's arm. "They seemed very friendly at first."

"They just didn't understand that you don't go around eating people just because you haven't had the chance to get to know them." Prunella sighed. "Some people have no table manners. We'll go in through the east gardener's gate. No one should see us there, and if they do, we'll say we're going to play tag among the standing stones."

The group moved quickly along the sidewalk, slowing only when Rohan tripped. It was hard to walk when your head was being held under someone's arm. Eventually, with Rohan's solemn promise never to threaten her with mud again, Ketiwe let him go. They came to a small gate in the wall. It was about four feet wide, with a small arch over the top. The gate was made of thick wood bound with iron slats. It made no noise when it was opened. Old though Strange House might be, it and its grounds were kept in good condition.

The children followed a narrow, winding path towards the house. On either side of the path were flower beds overgrown with roses. About every twenty feet along the path was a rose covered trellis. Pink and white clematis were also visible among the roses. Bees were everywhere, but were so busy gathering pollen they ignored the kids.

Denis moved up next to Prunella. "Why is the garden such a mess? I thought you had gardeners here to keep things tidy."

Prunella smiled. "If you could see the garden from the roof, you'd see that it's not really messy at all. It's an English country garden. There are no straight lines anywhere, and things are planted all over. There are vegetables next to flowers; things are planted where they'll look nice and where they'll like their neighbours. See that little green plant with the white flowers?" She pointed at a spot near a rose bush. "That's garlic. Roses are especially vulnerable to vampires."

"This garden is closer to nature than those places with vast amounts of grass." The gang looked at Julia as she bent and sniffed a rose. A bumble bee on a nearby bloom rose up, hovered around her head as if examining her for pollen, and then flew to the flower she had just sniffed. "See, everyone and everything gets along much better here."

"Alright, quiet now." Prunella held a finger to her lips. "We're at the side door."

Above the children, Strange House loomed like a quiet giant. The windows were set deep into the walls, covered with gables. Turrets sprang up all over the roof and cast long, finger-like shadows on the grounds next to the house. A slight breeze whistled through the many carvings on the walls. A pair of gargoyles peered down at the youngsters from the roof. Above the door, the sunny face of John Barleycorn smiled welcome to the house.

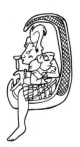

CHAPTER FOUR

The children huddled together just inside the side door. There was an alcove to the left where they could hang their coats. To the right was a narrow door, with a narrow and steep staircase visible behind it.

"That's the back way to the library. We can't go that way because I think Uncle Archie is there writing an article about the abominable snowman." Prunella motioned to the others to follow. "Keep close to the walls and step lightly. Mohan Singh could be anywhere."

"Lurking in the shadows?" asked Selamawit.

"No, Sela," replied Prunella, "he doesn't lurk so much as just appear. When he was in the army with Uncle Archie, Mohan could walk over piles of dead leaves and not make a sound."

"Just like Cain in Kung-Fu! Can he do martial arts too?" Denis got closer to Prunella, his face aglow with interest.

"I don't know for sure, but I bet he'd tell you all about it if you're willing to listen to him talk about his music too."

"What music? Does he play an instrument?" This time it was Selamawit who was interested.

"He can play the sitar, but he's more interested in this ancient music from something called the British Invasion. He's always talking about someone named Manfred Mann and how he's going to write the best book ever on him."

"Eek!" Rohan, who had moved a little ahead of the group, came tiptoing back very quickly. "It's Mohan Singh. He's coming this way! We're doomed!"

"Calm down and lean flat against the side of the staircase. Maybe he won't see us. It sometimes works in the movies."

Prunella and the others flattened themselves against the wood panelling on the side of the staircase. The banister cast a shadow over them that made them almost invisible to anyone no closer than twenty or so feet.

All 195 pounds of Mohan Singh was compacted into his five-foot five frame. His stern face was surrounded with jet black hair and long sideburns. Two deep brown eyes stared at some papers he was carrying as he climbed the stairs. The kids didn't notice the slight grin on his face as he moved. "There they were just a walkin' down the street, singin' do wah diddy diddy dum diddy do," he sang.

"Okay, he's gone." Prunella looked up the stairs after Mohan with puzzlement on her face. She shook her head, as if to clear her thoughts. "Come on, we'll take the small stairs on the other side of the house."

The six children moved as one past the staircase, through the main entrance hall, and down another corridor. They came to another narrow door behind which was a narrow staircase. Prunella pointed up. They went. After a few minutes, they came out in a heavily carpeted hall. There were chests of drawers and cabinets along the walls, and pictures and artifacts hung all over. It seemed that every ten feet there was another door.

"This way," beckoned Prunella and the gang followed her. They turned left and found themselves in another hall that looked just like the one they had left. "It's around the corner, I think."

"Don't you know for sure, Nell?" asked Denis.

"Hey, you've seen how many rooms and halls there are." Prunella replied, a little defensively. "It can get confusing in here. I once spent an hour trying to get back to my room after I had gone to the bathroom. And the bathroom was right next to my room."

They finally came to a heavy wood door that had a large green mask on it. The mask was made of hundreds of tiny

green pieces of some kind of stone.

"It looks like jade," said Rohan. "I saw a mask that was a little like this at a museum when I lived in New Delhi. That one was made of jade."

"I've seen masks like this too," said Julia quietly. "They're usually used in religious rituals. This one is beautiful."

"Let's go in," said Prunella as she reached forward and grasped the big brass doorknob.

The room was not very small, but it was crowded with stuff. There were low cabinets on which sat small statues and pieces of pottery. Showcases had insects pinned to cards with Latin names written on them in a fine script. The walls were covered with framed drawings of buildings in jungles. All the pictures were signed "Catherwood." One wall was covered with brightly coloured clothes, headdresses adorned with feathers and capes with finely embroidered designs. In one cabinet, there were several daggers that appeared to be made of black glass, and arrow heads of the same material. In the corners of the room were four large palm trees in colourful pots. The room seemed warmer than the hallway, as if to reflect the jungles in the drawings.

"Look what I've found," said Denis, holding up a large black ball. "It's made of some kind of woven stuff, but it weighs a ton. I read that the Maya played a game with a ball like this. It was like soccer and basketball combined, I think."

The group listened intently to Denis as he spoke. They had been "oohing" and "aahing" until then, marvelling at the treasures in the room.

"Hey, look here." Rohan was standing next to a large carving of a feathered serpent. "I didn't notice this door before, when we came in."

Prunella and the others moved towards Rohan. "This house is like that. One minute there's a solid wall, then suddenly there's a doorway. New hallways seem to pop up all over, too. Let's have a look."

Rohan pulled the door open to reveal a dark hallway. There seemed to be a slight warm breeze coming from within.

"Shall we?" asked Prunella.

"Ladies first," said Rohan, as he motioned the others through into the darkness.

CHAPTER FIVE

"Did anyone think to bring a flashlight?"

The group stood in almost total darkness. A sliver of light was still visible off in the distance, marking the entrance to the Maya room in Strange House. No one answered Prunella's question.

"Okay, new rule. From now on, anytime we go on an adventure, we go prepared. Please record that in the rule book, Mr. Secretary." Prunella's voice registered just the slightest bit of frustration. She hated delays.

Denis spoke up. "I didn't bring the rule book. Even if I had, I wouldn't be able to see to write anything down. And since when do we even have a rule book?"

"Every group has a rule book, it's a rule," said Prunella.

"Where I come from, we all just know the rules," said Julia.

"You're lucky," answered Prunella, "but we don't come from there. People around here are used to having everything written down in very complicated language that only lawyers can understand."

"Then what's the use of having them?" asked Ketiwe.

"My dad says it keeps the lawyers busy and out of normal people's hair," replied Rohan. "My dad meets a lot of lawyers at the Embassy and he doesn't have much hair."

"And we don't even have a name," said Denis. "Every decent group has a name."

"How about The Famous Five?"

"There are six of us."

"The Secret Six?"

"Been used."

"The Club of Babysitters?"

"Do you do any babysitting? I don't."

"Gupta?"

"Gupta? What kind of name is that?"

"I have an uncle who lives in Calcutta. He's a nice man."

"No, we have to have a dramatic name. Something that will make our enemies cower at the very mention of it."

"What enemies? We don't have enemies."

"It doesn't matter. It just has to be a name with power."

"What about The Strange Crew. We hang out at Strange House."

"That sounds like a rap group. Why not The Strangers?"

"Excellent! All in favour."

There was a chorus of "yeas."

"Any further business? No? Then I propose we go for something to eat."

"This is getting us nowhere. We have a name but still no light. Wait," Prunella patted herself down until she came to one of the lower pockets on her safari jacket. "We're in luck, I've got some matches."

"You should not be playing with matches. Only you can prevent forest fires."

"Thank you Selamawit the fire ranger," said Prunella with mild sarcasm. "They're left over from the holiday. I had them for lighting the fireworks we set off by the river on Sunday night. Let's see."

There was a scraping noise and suddenly the tunnel was lit by the flame of a match. The children found themselves in a long tunnel lined with massive stones. There were intricately painted animals and people all over the walls. Little square pictures, Denis identified them as glyphs, formed vertical columns every few feet. The glyphs told a story, said Denis, just like in the pyramids in Egypt.

"Ouch!" screamed Prunella. "The match burned down to my fingers." She lit another. "Now, pay more attention. Does that look like a door up ahead?"

They moved forward, and came to a large stone door, also covered with glyphs.

"Does it open?" asked Rohan.

Julia stepped forward and pressed her hands against the sides of the door. It started to move a little, then swung back into position.

"Give me a hand with this," she said. "It's heavy but the hinges seem well-oiled."

Rohan and Ketiwe put their shoulders to the door and it swung open on a central pivot to reveal a small chamber lit by torches. The Strangers moved into the chamber quietly, awed by the grandeur of the place. It was about twenty feet high and about thirty feet long and maybe fifteen feet wide. No one had thought to bring a tape measure. In the middle of the room was a huge stone block covered with carvings of men and women with ornate headdresses. Set on top of the block was what appeared to be a lid, beautifully carved with the figure of a man who seemed to be in a spacecraft's cockpit.

"We're in Pacal's tomb in Palenque," whispered Denis. "It's even more beautiful than in the pictures."

"Was he a spaceman?" asked Rohan, pointing to the carving.

"No," said Denis as he moved closer to get a better look at the carving. "He was a great Maya king. This is his sarcophagus, er, coffin, and that carving shows him descending into the underworld to battle the gods. Some people think it shows a spaceman flying a ship. They think ancient astronauts came to earth and showed people how to build pyramids."

"You know everything, Denis," said Selamawit.

"My special project for Miss Kane's class was on the Maya. Pacal was the most famous Maya king, so there was a lot of stuff about him in the books. Those people around the coffin are his ancestors. I don't know everything. Just most." He added, smiling.

"Hey, there's another door here," called Ketiwe from the top of some high stairs. "Do you want to see where it goes?"

"It should lead to a staircase up to a temple," said Denis as he moved to the door.

He and Ketiwe pushed at the door. "It's stuck, give us a hand." The others rushed up the stairs and put their backs to the job. With a loud cracking sound, the door swung open. Bits of half dried plaster fell from around the door and smashed on the floor.

"Uh oh," muttered Denis under his breath. Only Prunella noticed.

"What is it, Denis?" she asked quietly.

"Keep the others here for a moment while I check something out." He grabbed one of the torches and went through the door. He returned in a few seconds, his face quite pale. "Prunella," he said quietly, "when we go through the door, make sure everyone stays to the right and doesn't look back. I'll try to block the way."

"What is it?" she asked, a look of worry crossing her face.

"Nothing, much. It's just a bit gross."

"Right then! Is everyone ready to see more of this place?" Prunella pointed towards the door. "Up and to the right." She moved to the door.

Denis stood at the edge of the door blocking everyone's view of what lay behind it. He held the torch away from him, casting a shadow over what was behind the door. As she passed Denis, Julia looked him in the eye. He could tell she was aware of what lay behind the door, but she said nothing, as was her way. When everyone was through, Denis followed them up the stairs. As Denis passed her, Prunella took a quick look back. In the flickering light she could see feet sticking out from behind the door. There seemed to be at least three pairs, and they were stained with something dark. Prunella felt a cold finger run down her spine and shivered.

CHAPTER SIX

The stairs were high and steep. After a few seconds, they came to a landing. Everyone stopped to rest. The air was getting much warmer and the humidity was making everyone sweat.

After a short rest, they moved up the next flight of stairs. As they rose higher, they could see light from above.

"At least it's daytime," said Prunella. "We won't need those flashlights we forgot."

The gang emerged from the staircase into a large room, painted white. On a wall near the entrance to the staircase were more brightly painted carvings, or reliefs, as Denis called them. Through a doorway in the centre of the room, sky was visible. The children moved towards the outside, passing more walls covered with painted reliefs.

"This is called The Temple of Inscriptions because of all these reliefs," said Denis. "I didn't realize how badly they had been damaged by the weather and souvenir hunters."

"They seem to be in perfect shape now," said Prunella, "almost as if they had been finished yesterday." She moved closer to Denis. "What about what was behind the door downstairs?"

"Quiet!" he hissed. "I don't want to worry the others, yet. Let's just wait and see what happens."

They all moved through another doorway to the outside. Ketiwe, who was enthralled by a relief near the staircase entrance, lingered behind.

"Wow!" they said in unison.

"Palenque," said Denis in a hushed voice.

Below them stretched a red and white city. Stone buildings were everywhere, covered with reliefs and painted with every bright colour in the rainbow. Below and to their right was a large complex with a high tower, the only tower they could see.

"That's the Palace," said Denis.

Further to their right, they could see a fast flowing river and an aqueduct. Away from the plaza were dozens, maybe hundreds, of small wooden houses. They were clustered in little groups and around them were gardens, many with what appeared to be green fences. There were also lots of larger stone houses with high roofs. Next to these were small buildings with thatched roofs. Many of the larger houses were built on low stone mounds.

"The small houses are where the regular folks live. The bigger ones are for the nobility. Those little thatched buildings are the kitchens." Denis seemed to be in a trance. "It's as if my project has come to life."

In the distance, dissolving into the sunny haze, were plains, greener than anything they had ever seen.

"Where exactly are we?" asked Selamawit.

Denis replied, still in awe of the sight he beheld. "Palenque is in Mexico, in the skinniest bit. Below the Yucatan Peninsula."

"Is it far from Cozumel?" asked Prunella. "I went there for a vacation with my parents a few years ago."

"It's further south, more on the Gulf of Mexico side. I think maybe four hundred miles away."

People were everywhere, bustling about, moving from building to building. They were mostly dressed in plain white tunics with some colourful designs, but many were wearing elaborate capes and headdresses. Some seemed to be carrying weapons.

"Maybe they won't notice us," said Denis.

"Why not?" asked Rohan.

"I'm not sure this is the best time to be here. They may

not be ready for visitors."

"Hey, it looks like the natives have spotted us," said Prunella.

Down below, several people had stopped and were pointing to the top of the Temple where the Strangers stood. Some of the more ornately dressed men beckoned to some of the men with weapons and then ushered them towards the Temple. As the men reached the bottom of a long flight of steps that ran up the centre of the Temple, Prunella turned to the others.

"It might be a good idea if we made ourselves scarce. They don't look too friendly."

As they turned to run back into the Temple, three men emerged from within, waving spears with gleaming glass heads. There was nowhere to run.

CHAPTER SEVEN

The glass spear points were inches from their chests. The men, they must have been soldiers, nodded towards the stairs leading down from the Temple. The men's faces and arms were covered with tattoos and decorative scars which made them look fierce. Though the children were prisoners, the soldiers were clearly wary of them and tried to keep their distance with the spears. As they made their way down the stairs, Prunella looked around. Before them was a wide plaza, with a floor that looked like it had been painted white. Far off to the right, across the river, lots of men were working on a construction project. They seemed to be making small hills with brick borders. Across the plaza was another Temple built on a series of terraces, like steps.

The plaza itself was jammed with people. Everyone seemed to be stocky and very short, not much taller than the Strangers. The men had long black hair and most bore tattoos or scars similar to the soldiers. They wore breechclouts and capes, mostly red and white with complicated designs woven in. The women wore simple skirts and short tunics called huipiles. Some wore chemise and some, those who seemed to be more upper class, wore skirts down to their ankles. Many wore their hair plaited into two braids that were joined at the bottom; others had elaborate beehive hairdos or curls. The men wore leather sandals, the women were barefoot. Most of the children seemed to be hidden away.

One particularly striking aspect of many of the people was their foreheads. They looked flattened and went straight back from their noses to high on their heads. They almost had pointy heads. Most unusual.

Many people were working at stalls selling food, pottery, jewellery, and animals. Everyone appeared to be having a good time and Prunella decided they must be having some kind of carnival or festival. But where were the rides?

A large crowd had gathered at the base of the Temple. As Prunella and the others reached the bottom, the crowd parted to allow them to pass. They were herded to the Palace where a group of men in feathered costumes stood at the top of wide steps that went almost the whole length of the building. As the Strangers passed the Palace, the men moved along the side of the building watching them. They all turned to the right and came to more wide stairs that led up to a veranda.

"What do you think they want with us?" asked Rohan. "They don't seem very friendly."

"They're probably just curious," said Denis. "We look weird to them. Imagine if a posse of cowboys came to your village in India."

"We'd have made them welcome and asked them in for tea. That's what civilized people do, isn't it?" Rohan looked to the others for support.

"Let's give them a chance," said Prunella.

They were stopped at the top of the steps. The crowd of feathered men parted and they saw a man sitting cross-legged on a bench. The bench, made out of stone, had cats' heads carved on each side. The man had long black hair that flowed loose over his shoulders. Woven into his hair were small bits of jade and shell. His forehead was flat and sloped, but somehow misshapen, almost lumpy. His jaw was very large. From beneath his brows deep brown crossed eyes regarded the Strangers. He didn't seem to be afraid of them, unlike everyone else. His long robe glinted in the sun from the many iridescent feathers that had been woven into it. In his right hand, he held a sceptre with a double serpent head; in his left was a sceptre with a jaguar head.

"I think he's the king," said Denis, "maybe Chan-Bahlum,

Pacal's son. He sure looks noble."

As Prunella got closer, the man reached up and touched her hair, winding his large fingers through the red curls.

"Chac," he said.

"Haven't you ever seen red hair before?" she asked, smiling.

The man let her hair go and turned his eyes to the others. He rose and walked to Denis and Selamawit. He was well over six feet tall, a giant among the Maya.

"Oh wow, he's got six toes," exclaimed Rohan. "And six fingers. He must be a handy kind of guy."

Chan-Bahlum put his hand to Selamawit's face, rubbed her cheek, and looked at his hand.

He smiled, revealing filed teeth with golden inlays, and said, "Chiki."

"No sir, your highness," replied Selamawit. "I would never be cheeky to one so great as you."

Then he noticed Julia. He began to speak to her but she couldn't understand a word he said.

"Maybe they think you're from around here," said Rohan, "since you look a lot like them, except for the forehead."

"The Maya used to flatten children's foreheads. It's supposed to be a symbol of beauty or something," added Denis. "Same thing with the crossed eyes and the big nostrils." Many of the Maya had pieces of something stuck up their noses making their nostrils flare out.

"I suppose some of my people from Arizona may have come down this way at some time in history," said Julia. "I don't recognize any of the words they're saying."

As the man got to Rohan, who backed away nervously, he noticed the ball in Rohan's hands. He pointed to it and spoke some words to one of the feathered men. This man consulted with a few others and then nodded to the King. The King put his arm around Rohan's shoulder, which made Rohan's eyes bug out, and motioned to the other Strangers to gather round. He turned to the crowd in the plaza which until now had been silent. Raising his arms in the air, the King began to speak. Every now and then he would point at one of the kids and repeat "chac" or "chiki". Finally, he took the ball from Rohan, held it aloft and shouted something that sounded like "sheebalba" and then "pok-to-pok." The crowd erupted into cheers. There were smiles all over.

Prunella turned to Denis and said, "Yeah, right on, okay, what'd we do?"

Denis shook his head. "You've got me, but I think we may be honoured guests."

"They are not going to eat us then?" asked Selamawit. "We are not going to be put in more big pots?"

"I think not," said Prunella. "It looks like they want us to go in."

The Strangers followed the King into the Palace to whatever fate awaited them.

CHAPTER EIGHT

Fate decided to be kind to the Strangers, at least for the time being. They had been led through the Palace courtyard to a small room with a doorway and window that faced the Temple of Inscriptions. The room was all white with detailed and colourful paintings on every wall. Even the high ceiling had paintings - flying serpents with rainbow feathers, suns and stars and moons. There were no lights, but the door and window were wide enough to make it seem like daytime inside.

Rohan had been most excited by the hammocks. "Way cool, " he had shouted as he leapt into the one closest to him. "Not so cool," he had grunted when the hammock had flipped over and deposited him on the stone floor.

Now the group sat in a circle on the floor, trying to figure out what to do.

"It's something to do with the ball game," said Denis. "You saw how the King got all excited when he found the ball that Ro was holding."

"What's so special about a ball game anyway?" asked Prunella. "It's not like we came all this way to play games."

"Games are very important to my people. They have much religious significance." Julia spoke for the first time since they had entered the room. "Everything is important here."

"I think Julia's right," said Denis. "We've arrived during a sort of festival, I think. If that is Chan-Bahlum, then he's only just become king and may still be going through all the rituals of succession."

"What do you mean?" asked Rohan, who was leaning to one side, being careful to avoid the part of his backside that had cushioned his fall from the hammock.

"In the tomb, when we opened the door to the staircase, all that plaster fell on us. I think the tomb had just been sealed up. The old king, Pacal, may have only been buried a little while before."

"But why were there the torches burning in a sealed tomb?" asked Selamawit. "No one would need the light."

"The king would," said Julia, "to light his way to where ever his gods live. There was food there too, to ease his hunger on the journey."

"It tasted good," chimed in Rohan, "especially the thing like a taco." He looked at the others who were staring at him in amazement. "What? It was only one taco and a few beans. I was hungry."

"I'm sure a king as great as Pacal would be willing to share his food with another traveller," said Julia.

"Anyway, what about what was behind the door?" asked Prunella.

Before Denis could answer, they heard bells ring and several young Maya entered the room. Each one carried a large flat basket, like a serving tray, on which food was laid out. They placed the food on the floor in the middle of the circle formed by the Strangers. The servers were careful to keep their eyes averted. Julia leaned over and touched one of them, a boy, on the arm. He screeched and flinched back with a look of fear on his face. The others ran from the room.

Julia smiled at him and said, "Don't worry, I don't bite." She held her right hand forward, palm up. "I'm hoping he might take this as a friendly gesture." The boy looked at her hesitantly, looked at her hand, then smiled and held out his right hand, palm up. "I don't know what this means, but we may have just made a friend."

"Good for us, let's eat." Rohan eased forward and began to take food from the trays.

"Wait for it, Ro," said Denis impatiently, "This is more important. Besides, you've already eaten."

"Alright, if you say so," huffed Rohan. He moved back, a sour look on his face. Selamawit patted him on the shoulder and passed him a monstera, a fruit with a hexagonal shape. He grinned and began to eat it, savouring its flavour, a cross between pineapple, mango and banana.

"Try to find out if he knows anything about what's going to happen to us," said Prunella.

Julia pointed to the group and then to the ball lying on the floor next to Rohan. She shrugged. The boy looked at the ball then moved over to the doorway. He pointed at the Temple of Inscriptions, pointed at the floor, then at the Strangers.

"Sheebalba," he said. "Pok-to-pok."

He made a fist and thumped his chest over his heart. His eyes closed and his head tilted to one side. Then lifted his hands into the air and pointed to the Strangers.

"Nuts," said Denis, "I think I know what's going on."

"It has something to do with what was behind the door, doesn't it." As she said this, Julia leaned over and picked up the ball.

"Yes," said Denis. "Behind the door were the bodies of some people who were sacrificed so they could accompany the dead king on his journey. They would have had knives thrust into their hearts."

Selamawit jumped to her feet. "I thought that you said these were nice people. There would be none of this eating visitors or killing strangers."

"No, no, don't worry, I don't think they're going to kill us." Denis had gone over to Selamawit to calm her. "It's possible they think we are those sacrifices come back to life. There were five of them lying there. I think, because Rohan was carrying the ball, that they believe the dead were revived by the gods and sent back here to play a ritual game of ball. We're sort of celebrities."

"No killing?" asked Selamawit. "No eating people."

"Not that I can see," answered Denis. "But I am hungry now, let's eat."

They all sat down again. The Maya boy watched for a few seconds, then he slipped out the door. On the platters in front of the kids were several piles of tortillas, still steaming from being cooked. They had different flavours from being made of several types of corn. There were beans, spiced and hot, sweet potatoes, spaghetti squash, and nuts. In addition to the monstera, there were guavas and sugar apples. Small pots held meat and vegetable stews.

"Whatever you do," said Prunella seriously, "don't drink the water."

Rohan, who had been eating heartily, suddenly put down his food. "I just thought of something," he said, a look of horror spreading across his face. "What happened to Ketiwe?"

The Strangers all stopped eating then.

CHAPTER NINE

The Strangers all jumped up and hurried to the door.

"We've got to find her," cried Rohan, "she might get dirt on her clothes or something."

Prunella looked at him and frowned. "That's the least of her worries. What if she gets lost in the forest or taken to another part of the city? There's no one here we can ask for help."

As the children were about to step through the door, two guards appeared and levelled their spears across the space. They had stern looks on their faces and the spears were very sharp.

"We have to find our friend," said Rohan.

"They don't understand you, Rohan," said Julia. "Try not to annoy them."

Rohan backed away from the guards and almost tripped over the ball. He looked down at it, grunted, and gave the ball a good hard kick. The ball bounced off the back wall of the room and sailed through the doorway, over the lowered spears, and out into the plaza.

One of the guards moved to the middle of the doorway, with his spear pointed directly at the children. The other guard ran off in the direction of the Palace courtyard. The children milled around, frustrated at not being able to get out of the room.

"What do we do now?" asked Selamawit.

"There's not much we can do except wait," replied Prunella.

"Wait, look," cried Rohan. "The King is coming this way!"

They all looked out to see Chan-Bahlum moving hastily towards their room. He was followed by a large entourage of brightly dressed men. Several soldiers flanked the group.

"I don't like the look of this," said Prunella. "They don't look happy."

"We had better not be eaten now," said Selamawit. "I am not in the mood for this."

"The King is smiling, and he's carrying the ball." Denis turned to Julia. "Any ideas?"

Julia didn't have a chance to reply because the King came into the room at that point. The children all turned to look at him. He was still smiling and beckoned them to follow him. They left the room and went down some steps onto the plaza. There were still lots of people around, though not the crowd that had gathered when the Strangers had first been brought to the Palace. Most had gone back to whatever they had been doing before the appearance of the Strangers at the Temple. Several women were sitting on the ground weaving. Their looms were attached at one end to poles, the other end was strapped around their waists. They chatted happily as they wove their intricate designs. As they passed the people in the plaza, the Maya stopped whatever they were doing and stared at the children. Most had a look of awe on their faces. Many smiled and nodded their heads.

"It's that hair of yours, Nell," said Denis. "There's something special about red to the Maya. It symbolizes the east and sunrise. They use a ground up red mineral called cinnabar to decorate the inside of coffins."

Prunella glared at him. "What are you saying? That I've got mineral hair? Coffin head?"

Denis backed away and bumped into Rohan. "Geez," he muttered, "it's not like I was trying to insult her or anything. It's a good thing I didn't mention the ground up insects that make the red dye. Girls!"

"I know what you mean," said Rohan, "but at least she

didn't put you in a headlock."

As Rohan said this, they all moved around to the front of the Palace. Across the plaza, about half way to another set of temples, was a weird looking structure that looked like a small street. On either side of the street was a low building that resembled the stands at the soccer field back home.

They stopped at one end of the structure. The King stood and spread his arms wide to encompass everything.

"Pok-to-pok!" he shouted.

"The ball court," said Denis. "Wow, back in our time, it's just two mounds with some bits of stone sticking out. It hasn't been excavated yet."

As they all moved onto the ball court, they could see it was covered with brightly painted reliefs just like every other building in the city.

"Where are the seats?" asked Selamawit.

"There aren't any," replied Denis. "The spectators sit at the top of the two side buildings and look down into the central alley. They don't get too close to the action, I guess."

"The games are sacred," added Julia, "so the people keep a respectful distance."

The playing surface of the ball court was white stone, each slab fitted together so perfectly that there appeared to be no seams. A wall rose a few feet at the sides and then the surface sloped gradually for about fifteen or twenty feet to where the spectators sat. At the midpoint of the court, about half way up the slopes on each side, there were large stone rings, serpents devouring their tails.

"Those are the goals," said Denis, pointing to the rings. "The object is to get the ball through them."

"Hah, easy," said Rohan as he picked up the ball that the King had dropped. He tossed the ball at one of the rings, but it bounced off the side of the building and rolled away to the far end of the court.

One of the brightly dressed men ran over to Rohan and slapped his wrist.

"Ouch, hey, what's the idea?" Rohan stared at the man who bowed his head and backed away.

"I don't think you're supposed to use your hands, Ro," said Julia. "Look at the carvings."

The children moved along the low wall and saw what Julia meant. There were reliefs showing men dressed in padded equipment and playing a game. They appeared to use only their knees and hips to move the ball.

"It looks hard," said Prunella. "I can throw a baseball accurately, but I don't know about kneeing a soccer ball through a hoop."

"Take a look at these last carvings." Julia was on her knees at the far end on the court. The carvings seemed to tell the story of the ball game in some kind of order, and Julia was a faster reader than the others. "This doesn't look good."

The Strangers gathered round Julia.

"See this," she pointed to one of the carvings. "One of the players has scored a goal. In the next one, it looks like a team has won the game and the losers are being led away. One of them is tied up. The captain maybe." She moved along to the next carving. "This is the part I don't like. This man with all the feathers, he sort of looks like the King over there. He's sticking a knife in the captain of the losing team."

"You mean if we lose this game, we are going to be sacrificed." Selamawit looked angry.

"Not all of us," said Julia as she got to her feet, "just the captain."

"Mr. Secretary, the Strangers need to elect a leader."

CHAPTER TEN

"What do you mean I win again?" shouted Prunella.

"It was a fair and democratic election," replied Secretary Denis. "Just like the other three times."

Pieces of paper littered the floor of the Strangers' room in the Palace. Prunella stormed from one end of the room to the other, waving her arms in the air and yelling at space. Selamawit and Julia were sitting against one of the walls, and Rohan, having mastered the delicate process of getting on, was lying in a hammock. Denis stood in the middle of the room holding a pencil and the remains of a small notebook. The notebook had been used for ballots.

"Can we have another vote?" asked Prunella as she passed Denis again. "Maybe someone else will win this time."

"The only reason anyone else is getting any votes," said Julia quietly, "is because you are voting for them. So far you've voted for everyone but yourself."

Prunella stopped her pacing and stared at Julia. "I thought this was supposed to be a secret ballot!" she shouted.

"You're so obvious, Prue," said Julia. "Why don't you just calm down and try to think of a way out of this mess."

Prunella glared at Julia. "The name is Prunella, not Prue, Prunella. P.R.U.N.N.E.L.L.A. Prunella. Got it?"

"You spelt it wrong," said Rohan from his hammock. "I think you put in too many Ns."

"Are you saying I can't spell my own name?" screamed Prunella as she moved quickly towards Rohan.

Rohan's eyes popped open and he tried to sit up. This only caused the hammock to start rocking and then flip over, dumping Rohan onto the hard floor.

"My bum!" cried Rohan.

"That is B.U.M." said Selamawit.

Prunella stopped and turned to look at Selamawit. She stared for a few moments then burst out laughing. Cautiously at first, the others joined in Prunella's laughter.

"Well, I guess it is my house and we are sort of named after me."

"Whoa! We only elected you captain of our doomed ball team, not Queen of Everything," gasped Denis as tears began to roll down his face. Once Denis started to laugh, it was often very hard to get him to stop.

"Sorry. Sometimes I act so strange," said Prunella, "but that's my name so don't wear it out. Now be serious, Denis." This only caused Denis to get the giggles. "We have to find a way out of this mess."

"I have to pee," said Rohan from the floor.

"What? What kind of suggestion is that?" Prunella looked over at Rohan who had climbed to his feet and looked very uncomfortable.

"Falling shook everything up," he said, "and now I have to pee. Where's the bathroom?"

"What do mean, Ro? You should have gone before we left. No one ever goes to the bathroom when they're having an adventure." Prunella looked to the others for confirmation of this. Some nodded. "Captain Kirk never has to pee. Neither does Indiana Jones."

"Well I'm not Captain Kirk or Indiana Jones," said Rohan defiantly. "I'm Rohan Chaudry and I need to go!"

He walked towards the doorway and the guard waiting there. The guard stepped back and tightened his grip on his spear. Rohan made some motions with his hands while the guard watched. The guard grunted, smiled and led Rohan away.

"Do you think that is the last we will ever see of Rohan?" asked Selamawit.

"He's just going to the bathroom," said Denis. "Why must everyone take everything so seriously?" He started to giggle again.

"We are in a serious situation," said Julia as she got to her feet. "Ketiwe is missing and one of us may end up getting sacrificed if we lose the ball game."

"Uncle Archie would know what to do, but I don't dare ask him for help again." Prunella let out a sigh.

The four of them paced around the room for a few minutes. Once in a while, one would stop, look up, and then start pacing again. Suddenly, Prunella let out a yell.

"I've got it," she started, "we just need to..."

"Guys, guys, you've got to see this." Rohan burst into the room. "They have really cool bathrooms, with urinals and everything!"

The others gathered round, interested.

"The bathroom's all white, just like everything else, and there are these neat paintings on the ceiling. Flowers and birds. And there are urinals and they flush."

"Way cool," said Prunella. She turned towards the guard at the door. "Hey mister, I have to pee."

"Me too," said Julia and Selamawit.

"Me first," said Prunella. "After all, I am captain."

The guard seemed a little overwhelmed by the girls and called to a guard at another door. A few seconds later, a woman appeared dressed in an embroidered huipile and a plain skirt. Her long black hair was tied back with ribbons. She led the girls away.

Denis and Rohan looked at each other and shrugged.

"Did anyone come up with a solution to our problem?" asked Rohan.

"Prunella was about to say something when you came in," answered Denis. "Funny how girls always have to go to the bathroom in groups like that. I just don't understand it."

"Me neither," said Rohan. "Maybe it makes them faster. Here they are already."

The girls ran back into the room giggling.

"So that is what a urinal looks like. They are very pretty," said Selamawit.

"They're not so fancy back home," said Prunella. "There they're more like skinny bathtubs standing on end."

"You've been in a men's bathroom?" asked Julia.

"Only once," said Prunella with a smile on her face, "when Tommy Lush called me a name and threw my textbook in the boy's washroom at school."

"Is that how Tommy's glasses were broken?" asked Denis.

"I wouldn't know," said Prunella innocently.

"Denis said you had come up with a solution to all our problems," Rohan piped in. "What's your plan?"

"Hah! It's so simple. One of us goes back through the tomb, out of Strange House, finds Jozef, and brings him back here. With his skills, we should win any old ball game."

Denis looked at Julia and Selamawit, who were frowning. "Oh yes, very simple, except for the fact that Ketiwe is still missing, and we are being held prisoner by thousands of Maya."

Denis threw his hands in the air. "So simple!"

"I said it was simple, I didn't say it was easy."

Rohan was standing over by the doorway. "Maybe we should get some rest. It's getting dark and it looks like it might rain."

"Good idea," said Prunella as she moved to stand next to him. "Maybe we'll be able to sneak out once everyone is asleep."

They each climbed into a hammock.

"Good night Denis."

"Good night Prunella. Good night Julia."
"Good night Denis. Good night Rohan."
"Good night Julia. Good night Selamawit."
"Good night Rohan. Good night John-Boy."
Snores soon filled the room. And that's when the shadow entered.

CHAPTER ELEVEN

Ketiwe stood before the relief by the staircase and stared at it. The fine detail was like nothing she had ever seen. Every feather on the winged serpent, every leaf on the tree was clear. She moved along the wall, noticed the small glyphs arranged in rows across the top and down in columns. She hadn't realized she was alone. At the sound of Prunella's voice, Ketiwe turned to join the others.

"It might be a good idea if we made ourselves scarce. They don't look too friendly."

What was that all about? Ketiwe wondered. *Who didn't look too friendly? Surely there weren't any people here.*

As she neared the doorway through which the others had passed, Ketiwe saw some odd looking shadows pass over the floor. She shrank back against the wall, arms pressed out at her sides, in the position designed to afford maximum invisibility. At least it did according to Prunella.

Ketiwe could hear some men yelling. *Men? What men?* She eased her head around the corner in time to see three men with wings descending a staircase.

Cautiously, Ketiwe crept through the doorway and peered round the corner. No one was in sight. She moved forward slowly and noticed people, quite a large crowd in fact. Immediately she fell to the floor in a crouch. Almost as quickly she reared up and looked at her hands to check for dirt from the floor. There was none. *Whoever these people are, they are clean.*

Crouching again, Ketiwe crept forward until she was between two of the columns at the front of the temple. Now she could see down the stairs while remaining in shadow. With a little luck, no one below would notice her.

At the bottom of the stairs were the other Strangers. They

were being led across a plaza to a beautiful white building to the right. The men with wings, Ketiwe could see now, just had ornate red-feathered headdresses. The feathers were so large they hung down to the men's waists. Those spears they were pointing at her friends didn't look too pleasant.

As she lay there watching, the Strangers were led around the corner to a side of the large building that Ketiwe couldn't see.

Now what do I do? she thought. *I must help them, but how? I'm all alone.*

As she was thinking this, two men in long flowing robes came up the stairs towards her. They were deep in conversation, so they didn't see her. Quickly, Ketiwe shuffled back behind the column, then along a corridor to a small room. A dead end! She was forced to wait until she could no longer hear the men speaking.

Quietly, Ketiwe moved to the column closest to her. She looked out at the plaza, still full of people, and tried to spot her friends. No luck, but at least the crowd down there seemed to be paying attention to something in the opposite direction from where Ketiwe stood. She eased her way around the column and moved to her right.

She could see that the temple was built on a series of terraces. Where she stood the terraces looked really steep. She could probably jump down them, but there was too much risk of being spotted by someone in the crowd. Ketiwe moved to the back of the temple. Here, a few levels down, the terraces were built right into the mountainside. There was thick jungle only a few feet from where she stood.

I don't think I have any choice, she thought. *I hope there are no creatures in there.*

Ketiwe climbed down two terraces until she came to a spot where a terrace met the slope of the mountain. The slope was covered with trees. There didn't seem to be much vegetation on the ground except right at the edge of the forest. The trees had huge trunks that went up so far, Ketiwe couldn't see the tops. A solid canopy of rich green leaves blocked out most of the sunlight. Vines hung down from the canopy and snaked their way around the trunks of the trees. She could only see ground for a few feet before it was swallowed up by darkness. She took a cautious step forward then ran like mad when she heard voices behind her.

It was much cooler under the trees, though still very humid. Ketiwe moved up the slope for several feet, until she could no longer see the temple. Then she began to move to the side, hoping to find a path or some way to get to her friends. The forest was silent but for the occasional calls of birds high in the trees.

A sudden movement further up the slope made Ketiwe halt and crouch down. Her eyes had adjusted to the darkness and she could make out something by a tree. She eased forward until she could lean on a tree trunk, then concentrated on what was up ahead. Something sleek and low was moving through the trees. It looked to be all grey in the absence of light, but Ketiwe could make out spots on its body. A jaguar, she thought, I hope he doesn't want to eat me. Just as she had that thought, the jaguar leapt forward and in an instant was gone. A few seconds later, Ketiwe heard a thump and a squeal.

As she breathed a sigh of relief, Ketiwe looked at the tree next to her. By her hand, which she had rested on the tree's rough bark, sat a huge spider, it's hairy front legs waving towards her outstretched fingers. She shrieked and pulled her hand away, threw herself off balance, and fell on her backside. She rolled a few feet and came to a stop against another tree. As she stood up, she brushed herself off, noting with disgust the stains on her once clean clothes. "Mr. Spider," she said calmly, looking at the creature as it made its way up the trunk, "it was not nice of you to startle me like that. Look at my clothes. Next time, you die!" She pulled a twig from her hair and tossed it at the spider, which ignored her and continued on its journey.

Ketiwe had seen the river that ran behind the large building where her friends had been taken. She decided to find this river and see if there was a path along it. After a few minutes, light began to filter through the canopy above. Ketiwe soon found herself looking down on the river. The trees on either side of it formed a sort of tunnel. Sunlight glinted off the water every now and then as a light breeze caused the leafy canopy to sway and create openings to the sky.

As she made her way down the slope towards the river, Ketiwe saw some tapirs drinking from the river's edge. They were reddish and looked a bit like cows except they were much shorter. As her feet crunched on some dead leaves, the tapirs looked up and then ran off in all directions, squealing like mad. Within seconds, there was no sign that the beasts had ever been there.

One of the cowardly animals had almost run head first into a small temple not far from the riverbank. There didn't appear to be anyone around, so Ketiwe crept up to the building in search of a clean place to sit and rest. A large snake slithered away from a sunny spot where it had been basking.

"I must think," she said quietly to herself, "all I've done so far is get further away from my friends."

She looked at her surroundings. There appeared to be nothing of any use around. A few baskets full of corn cobs sat by a wall. She sat down on the wall, after brushing away some dust, and drummed her fingers on the head of a man carved into a block of stone next to her.

Sitting there, trying to come up with a rescue plan, she ignored the occasional crack of twigs. It's probably some small animal trying to avoid the jaguar, she thought.

Then something tapped her on the shoulder.

CHAPTER TWELVE

Ketiwe had first tried out for the school wrestling team. Until then it hadn't been the "boys'" wrestling team because no one had ever expected a girl to try out for it. Soon after Ketiwe had tried out, there were three girls' wrestling teams in the city. The local school board had been anxious to avoid a lawsuit. Ketiwe, as everyone expected, was the city-wide champion. What was not as widely known was that she had already beaten every boy who had tried out for the Tyndale Junior High team. The coach, who had previously believed that girls should stick to girl's sports like cheer leading, had wanted Ketiwe on his team. He fought hard to keep her, but in the end he was forced to form a separate girls' team to keep the boys' fathers happy.

In less time than it takes to blink, Ketiwe had the person who had tapped her on the shoulder pinned to the ground with a deadly headlock. She looked down on the face of a Maya boy with deep brown eyes that were trying to pop out of his head. Despite the obvious fear on his face, the boy smiled showing lots of pearly white teeth. Suddenly there was a huge flower before Ketiwe's eyes, held there by the trembling hand of her prisoner.

"Typical boy," she hissed, "trying to get out of trouble with flowers." She let go of the boy's head. "It'll work this time, but you'd better not try anything funny."

She got to her feet as the boy rubbed his neck. As he struggled to get up, Ketiwe reached down, took his hand, and lifted him up. She sniffed the flower and looked at it closely. It was a gorgeous white bloom with pink spots down the middle of the petals. The bloom was as big as both of her hands together.

"My name is Ketiwe," she said, and pointed at herself.

"Ketiwe," she repeated.

The boy stared for a moment then pointed to himself and said, "Chan."

Suddenly, the boy grabbed her wrist and started to pull her towards the forest. He had a look of panic on his face. Ketiwe resisted him for a moment until she heard some voices approaching from along a path by the river. They moved behind the temple and up the slope to the edge of the forest. There was a large stone head sitting on a small outcropping of rock. The pair ran behind the head and crouched down.

The two watched a pair of soldiers pass their hiding spot and continue along the path. As they walked, they talked animatedly and laughed a lot. At one point, they stopped and one of them walked up to the small building. He picked up the flower that Ketiwe had dropped when she and the boy had run to hide. The soldier looked around, dropped the flower, and rejoined his companion. They began moving along the path again and soon passed out of sight.

After a few seconds, Chan tapped Ketiwe's arm and indicated that they could return to the temple.

"What am I going to do with you?" said Ketiwe to the boy. He looked at her without comprehension. "Wait a minute!"

She reached into her pocket and took out a wallet. She opened the wallet and pulled out a wrinkled photograph. After smoothing it out, Ketiwe showed it to Chan. It was a group shot of the Strangers, taken by Mohan Singh after their adventure with the Laplanders.

Chan's reaction was instant. His jaw dropped in amazement, then a huge grin appeared on his face. He spoke some words that Ketiwe couldn't understand and pointed in the direction of the big building where her friends had been taken. He moved his hands as if he was eating.

"They're being fed," said Ketiwe, "that should make

Rohan happy. But why were they taken away?"

Chan looked at her intently. She threw her hands up. Then the boy smiled and ran off. He came back quickly with a large round squash. He bounced the squash off his knees, then swung his hips and sent the squash soaring off into the river. The look on the boy's face told Ketiwe he had just made a mistake.

"Oops," she said to him, "but I think you mean my friends are going to play some kind of game. It must have been that ball that Denis found. Can you take me to them?"

She looked at Chan, who just looked back. She pointed to the photograph and then down the path towards her friends. Chan nodded and Ketiwe began to head towards the path, but Chan grabbed her and pulled her towards the temple.

They went into the temple and Chan disappeared into a small room off to the left. He returned a few moments later with a pile of clothes. He gave Ketiwe a short white skirt and a cape decorated with toads. She put them on over her own clothes and noticed that her jeans looked completely out of place, as did her running shoes. She rolled up her pant legs until they were hidden by the skirt, and took off her shoes and socks. She stuffed the socks in her shoes, after folding them neatly, tied the shoelaces together and strung her belt through the laces. With the cape over the skirt, the bulge made by her shoes was invisible.

"Ready?" she asked Chan.

He stared at her for a moment then touched her face gently.

"What's the matter? Is it my face?" She raised a hand to her cheek. "Of course! My skin is dark brown. How are we going to hide it?"

Chan ran into a different room. This time Ketiwe followed. She stopped dead as she entered the room and saw what was contained within. On a table by a window, a piece of paper, or something that looked like paper anyway, was laid out flat. Covering the top half of the paper were drawings of glyphs and, were those words? Next to some small clay pots were various brushes and feathers.

Ketiwe walked over to the table and picked up a pouch that was resting near the paper. Within she found more paper, folded like a fan and bound between two boards. As she looked around the room, she could see the walls were lined with shelves filled with books like the one she was holding.

"A library," she said quietly. There was a smile on her face. "This is a real treasure."

Meanwhile, Chan had taken a small pot from the table and removed its lid. He dipped his fingers in and they came out covered with a red paste. He moved towards Ketiwe.

"You are not going to put that stuff on me!" cried Ketiwe. "It's gross."

Chan frowned and raised an eyebrow as if to say, "Do you have a better idea?"

Ketiwe took a deep breath and sighed. "I suppose I don't have any choice. This adventure is just too dirty."

Chan smeared the red goo all over Ketiwe's face, then moved down to her legs and feet. When he was done, he stepped back and looked at her. He shrugged his shoulders and smiled. He was about to put the lid back on the pot when he said, "Ketiwe!" She was startled to hear her name from this strange boy. He pointed to her arms.

"But they're hidden by the cape," she protested.

Chan stood his ground and held out his hand. Ketiwe lifted her right arm to him and when he was finished, raised her left arm. The red goo dried very quickly and made her skin itch.

"I hope this stuff washes off easily."

Chan grabbed a brush and another pot. With a few deft strokes, he added some blue tattoos to Ketiwe's skin.

For a final touch, Chan produced a straw hat and plopped it on Ketiwe's head. From a distance, she looked just like a Maya girl.

They returned to the outside of the temple. Chan picked up one of the baskets of corn that was sitting by the wall. He gave it to Ketiwe, then picked up another basket. He tilted his head towards the path and started off.

"I hope this goes smoothly," said Ketiwe.

Chan hissed at her to be quiet. People were coming down the path. Ketiwe fell into step behind Chan and kept her head down. They passed people on the path, but no one seemed to take any notice of the two. After a short distance, far less than Ketiwe expected after her trip through the forest, they came to the side of the temple where the Strangers had entered the city. The path split into two, one heading to the left to join the plaza, the other going right towards a structure that looked like a low bridge.

As the two were about to turn left and head for the plaza, a group of about twenty soldiers appeared from around the front of the Temple of Inscriptions. Chan stopped dead, turned to face Ketiwe and nodded in the direction of the bridge thing. They moved quickly away from the soldiers, who ignored the youngsters and marched down the path.

"That was close," whispered Ketiwe. "What is that thing ahead of us?"

Chan stared at her, a frown on his face.

"Sorry, I keep forgetting, you don't speak English."

As they neared the structure, Ketiwe could see that it was connected to the river and passed close to the large building where she hoped her friends still were. She realized the thing was not a bridge but an aqueduct, drawing water from the river and taking it to the building. As she noted this, a man appeared from up ahead. They kept walking but the man shouted something in a harsh voice. She recognized Chan's name. They stopped and the man approached them. He did not look very friendly.

CHAPTER THIRTEEN

The man approached Chan and Ketiwe rapidly. As he neared them, his voice rose and the words he was saying seemed much harsher. Following Chan's lead, Ketiwe bowed her head and stared at the ground. The brim of her hat kept her face hidden from the man. She could hear Chan's voice, trembling yet slightly defiant. From her restricted field of vision, Ketiwe could see nothing of what the man was doing.

Ever so carefully, Ketiwe lifted her head, just enough to raise the hat brim so she could see Chan and the man. Chan was holding his basket of corn higher and the man was reaching into it, as if he was searching for something. The man looked up and over at Ketiwe.

I'm a dead girl, she thought. *He'll see I'm not a Maya and throw me in jail. I hope they don't torture people here.*

She quickly lowered her head again and saw the man's feet as he got next to her. She held her basket up for his inspection. The man reached in and swirled his hand around. Having not found whatever it was he was looking for, he grunted and backed away. Then Ketiwe saw that he was walking around her.

Sizing me up for a cell, she thought. *God, please stop my knees from shaking.*

Chan said some more things, his tone more determined than before. The man stopped circling Ketiwe and walked back over to Chan. He shouted something short and nasty sounding and stalked off.

Ketiwe suddenly realized that she hadn't been breathing since the man appeared. She took a deep breath and let it out slowly. *Thank you*, God. She looked up at Chan. He looked a little pale despite his bronze skin. He smiled at her, but it looked a little forced. He put down his basket. So did Ketiwe.

Chan smiled and looked in the direction the nasty man had taken. His smile turned to a frown. He grunted something that sounded like "too-peel-ob" and spat on the ground. Ketiwe repeated what Chan said and spat too. This surprised Chan, but made him smile again.

"Now what?" asked Ketiwe.

Sensing that she was asking a question, Chan nodded at the aqueduct and picked up his basket. He waited for Ketiwe to recover her basket, then they set off for the aqueduct. It was a low structure, maybe ten feet high, and Ketiwe could hear the water rushing along it.

The path ran beside the aqueduct for a few feet, then turned under it through a low arch. Chan followed this turn, but when they emerged on the other side, he turned left and moved along the side of the aqueduct rather than along the path towards the river. Between the aqueduct and the river were many beds of vegetables surrounded by prickly hedges. Ketiwe could see beans and some kind of squash closer to the river, but right next to the aqueduct was high corn. They moved through the corn until they came to a small alcove in the wall of the aqueduct.

Chan put down his basket and sat on a small rock at the back of the alcove. He gestured for Ketiwe to do the same, pointing to a rock close by his own. As Ketiwe sat, Chan pulled a small cloth sack from behind his rock and reached in. He produced a pair of corn cakes and passed one to Ketiwe. He then brought out a small pot of cold stew and dipped his corn cake in it.

Ketiwe hadn't realized how hungry she was. The corn cake was delicious by itself, but with some of the stew it was out of this world. Chan had a few more corn cakes in his bag and they were quickly eaten. Then Ketiwe remembered the chocolate bar in her pocket. She took it out and removed the wrapper, but in the heat it was a runny mess. Chan reached over and stuck a finger into the goo and tasted it. The smile on his face was the biggest Ketiwe had yet seen. She passed the whole bar over to him, being careful not to get any of the runny chocolate on her hands.

"So," she said, "is this your secret place? Are you a slave? No, you couldn't be after the way you spoke to that man. He's probably a corrupt official who doesn't like you but can't do anything about it. You must have something on him."

Through all this, Chan tried to pay attention, but he was too busy licking every trace of chocolate from the foil wrapper. When he was done, he examined the wrapper, trying to figure out what it was made of and how it worked.

"We can't leave anything behind," said Ketiwe as she reached over and took the wrapper from Chan. "It might mess with history. That's what Prunella's Uncle Archie says, and he should know."

She folded the wrapper carefully and put it in her pocket. Chan leaned back against the wall and stared out at the corn.

"When do we leave?" asked Ketiwe. She got up to go.

Chan grabbed her arm and pulled her back onto her seat. He shook his head. On the sandy floor he drew a circle with lines radiating from it.

"The sun," said Ketiwe.

The Chan drew a crescent moon and pointed to it.

"We have to wait for night," said Ketiwe. "That makes sense." She leaned back against the wall. "I hope we don't have to wait too long." Before she knew it, her eyes were closed.

When she awoke, it was dark outside the alcove and she was completely alone.

CHAPTER FOURTEEN

"Don't run out there in panic," Ketiwe said to herself. "You'll only get lost. Maybe eaten by a jaguar. Or worse, captured by that snotty man from this afternoon."

Slowly, Ketiwe crept to the edge of the alcove. Looking straight up, she could see the stars. There seemed to be no sign of anyone about so she slipped between the rows of corn and moved towards the path. *He'll come back that way,* she thought. *I hope.*

It had rained while Ketiwe had been sleeping and the soil between the corn rows was moist. She tried to avoid the wettest places, but when a sudden noise to her left startled her, she slipped on an exposed rock and slid into a large puddle. Grinding her teeth together, she suppressed the scream that ached to come out. A few tears escaped from her eyes, such was the strain of holding in her anger and frustration at being in the mud.

The noise to her left started up again. Ketiwe stood up, squeezed some of the water out of her skirt and scraped some mud off her legs. Now her hands were filthy, but she took care of those on a few convenient corn leaves. Quietly she moved towards the sound. After a few yards, the corn rows came to an end. Peering through the last row, Ketiwe could see down a path between two prickly hedges to the river. There, a small herd of cowardly tapirs were drinking. Across the river, she could see some Maya men working in torchlight on a construction project. They were building some more terraces. Nearby were some large blocks of stone.

As she watched, Chan walked through the construction site and crossed a small wooden bridge. The tapirs heard him, looked up, many snorted, and then ran off in a panic. Five or six of the beasts ran directly at where Ketiwe was hiding. As they thundered towards her, she remembered how they reacted to any unusual noise. She waited until they were only about ten feet away, then leapt up and screamed at them. Immediately the animals ground to a halt, great clods of earth flying into the air. In the blink of an eye, they scattered in all directions; some bounced off the hedges, squealed and disappeared into the night.

Meanwhile, Chan had come along the path from the river and detoured into the corn. He must have guessed that Ketiwe had scared the animals because he came straight along the row in which she was hiding.

"Where..." she began, but Chan put a finger to his lips and led her back to the alcove.

Before Ketiwe could ask more questions that Chan couldn't understand, he took some fresh clothes out of a small basket. There was a chemise and a skirt, but they were of much finer cloth than those which Ketiwe was wearing. The embroidery was more intricate, too. There were lots of green frogs and red diamonds. She quickly changed into these new clothes. Also in the bag was what appeared to be a wig. Chan put it on Ketiwe's head and wound a ribbon around it to keep it in place.

"As long as it's dark," she whispered, " no one should notice."

Chan indicated that she should follow him, and a finger to his lips told her that she should stay quiet. They moved along the side of the aqueduct until they came to another arch. Through this, they came to the foot of a short flight of stairs leading up to the large building where her friends were. Next to the stairs was a long low building. Smoke was billowing from a chimney at one end and light could be seen through a door at the other end. Chan approached boldly, as if he belonged there. Ketiwe followed.

They entered the door and Ketiwe was instantly hit by a variety of aromas. They were in a kitchen. A woman sat in a corner grinding some corn, and another two sat nearby making corn cakes from a big pot of dough. There were piles of vegetables everywhere. A woman took a large stone from a steaming pot of stew and placed it in a fire. The pot was then set down next to several trays of food by the door. Chan grabbed the pot and pointed at one of the trays. Ketiwe picked it up, smiled at the woman grinding the corn, and followed Chan out of the kitchen. Sweat was pouring down their faces. Warm as it might be outside, the kitchen was like an oven.

Chan led the way further into the building. They came to a long corridor, along which were posted several soldiers.

Remain calm, thought Ketiwe, *Chan knows what he is doing, even if I have only known him for a few hours and have no reason at all to trust him. Except that he is my friend and I must.*

As they passed the soldiers, comments were made. Chan replied with a happy voice and often the soldiers would start to laugh. Finally they came to a doorway and Chan stopped before the soldier who was guarding it. He spoke a few words, held up the pot of stew, and nodded over at Ketiwe, who quickly lifted her tray of food. She kept her face down. Despite the wig and the dim light from the torches, she didn't want to take the chance of the soldier noticing how different her face was. She hoped the red goo and the tattoos hadn't washed off when she fell into the puddle.

She could hear snoring from within the room. *That's got to be Julia*, she thought, *I'd recognize that sound anywhere.*

The soldier said something, grabbed a piece of fruit from Ketiwe's tray, and passed them through. Chan shook a small string of bells that hung by the doorway and pulled aside a blanket that was serving as a door. Ketiwe's knees were shaking as she went through.

The room was dark, silent and apparently empty. Chan and Ketiwe went to the middle of the room and placed the food on the floor. They turned to leave.

I thought my friends were in here, thought Ketiwe as fear began to set in, *Where are they?*

Suddenly there was a hiss, and a great weight bore Ketiwe to the floor.

CHAPTER FIFTEEN

There was a sudden crack! and a flash of light. Prunella had struck a match and the sight that she beheld was truly amazing. On the floor by the wall, Ketiwe was sitting on a blanket. Held tightly between her knees was Rohan's head. Under her left arm, Denis was held immobile, while under her right arm was Julia's head and Selamawit's left foot. Selamawit was trying to crawl away, but her foot was held in an iron grip.

Prunella looked down to see that she was sitting on a young Maya boy. Just before the match burned out on her fingers, she noted the look of pain on his face as she held his arm in a half nelson.

"Okay, nobody panic. I'm going to light a torch."

When the room was again lit, the scene hadn't changed.

"How did you light the torch without letting go of the boy's arm?" asked Denis, his voice slightly strained from Ketiwe's grip.

"Magic. Hello Ketiwe, long time no see."

Ketiwe ignored Prunella as she let go of her captives and helped them to their feet. They all stared at each other for a moment, then cheered and did a gang hug. Prunella remained seated on Chan.

"Quiet!" she hissed. "We don't want to alert the guards."

They all moved to the centre of the room and made a circle around the newly arrived food.

"I think she likes me a lot," Rohan whispered to Denis. "My neck will be sore for a week."

"Have something to eat, Rohan," Denis replied. "I think she likes me, too."

"No way," said Rohan between bites of fruit, "she likes me best. Check the dents in my head." Juice dribbled down his

chin. "Oops."

"So, where have you been, Ketiwe? We've been worried out of our minds." Prunella had moved into the circle. Chan was sitting next to her, his arm still locked behind his back, and a very sour look on his face. "And who's our friend here?"

"Please let him go," said Ketiwe. She moved next to Chan and took Prunella's hand from his arm. Gently, she rubbed Chan's arm and smiled at him. He smiled back but glared at Prunella.

"He's my friend; his name is Chan." At the sound of his name, Chan smiled to everyone and gave a small wave. "He helped me get here and keep out of the way of the bad guys."

"So, while we've been held prisoner..." began Prunella.

"And fed twice," interrupted Rohan.

"...and had our lives threatened..." Prunella continued.

"And been treated like gods, sort of," said Denis.

"...you've been out there..." Prunella went on, frustration beginning to show in her voice.

"But we have not been eaten by anyone," said Selamawit.

"...HAVING FUN WITH THE NATIVES." Prunella stopped herself.

"You think this is fun!" said Ketiwe harshly. "I've fallen in the forest dirt, slipped into a mud puddle, had red and blue goo smeared all over me, been attacked by wild beasts, and my clothes are a mess. This is not fun!"

"Would you like my hanky?" asked Rohan. He held it out to Ketiwe.

She took it with a smile. "Thank you," she said as she wiped her face. She looked at the white square and only saw some patches of brown dirt. "The red stuff didn't come off."

"You would like the bathrooms here," said Selamawit.

"The red stuff didn't come off," Ketiwe repeated to herself.

"There is running water," continued Selamawit, "and the toilets flush. They are spotless and very pretty."

Ketiwe's face brightened at this. "Let's go. I need."

"We'll worry about that later," said Prunella. "We need you to get help for us."

Prunella explained to Ketiwe all about the game and their role in it. Then she outlined her plan of escape.

"Maybe your friend, Chan, can help you get back to the Temple and then back to Strange House," said Denis.

Meanwhile, Chan had stood up and gone out the door. They could hear talking outside the room, and a few moments later, Chan returned. He tapped Ketiwe on the shoulder and pointed to the food tray and the pot and then outside.

"I think he means we have to take back the tray and pot before the guards get suspicious," said Ketiwe. "I'll get back as fast as I can."

"Don't forget to take something from this time with you," said Denis, "so you'll come back to the same time. There's no guarantee that there's anything else in the Strange House Maya room from exactly this year. You wouldn't want to end up coming back to Chichen Itza. Those Maya are not nearly as friendly as these ones."

With that, Ketiwe and Chan gathered up their loads and walked out the door. Ketiwe led the way, as if suddenly sure of where she was going.

"Now perhaps we should get some real sleep," said Julia.

"But why couldn't we all just sneak back to the Temple?" asked Rohan. "If Ketiwe can get out, then surely we can too."

"The guards would know how many people came in to feed us," said Selamawit. "They are not stupid men. Do not be afraid, Rohan. Ketiwe will get Jozef to help us. She is strong and brave, like the rest of us."

"Selamawit is right," said Prunella as she got into her hammock. "There's really nothing more we can do until Jozef gets here."

"I wonder when they'll arrive," said Denis.

"You mean they may not get back to exactly this time?" asked Julia.

"They probably will, but they could end up getting here yesterday or next week. We just don't know. Time travel is a very inexact science."

"Thank you, now I'll really be able to sleep," said Rohan just before he fell out of his hammock.

CHAPTER SIXTEEN

Something was crawling up Prunella's chest. Resisting the urge to jump up and flee, which would have been impossible since she was in a hammock, she eased one eye open. The thing now had its claws in her shoulder and she could feel small puffs of breath on her cheek. Not two inches from her eye was another eye, surrounded by brilliant green feathers.

Skrawwk!! it said, and leaned back from Prunella's face.

"Hello, Parrot," said Prunella, "you almost scared me to death."

The parrot continued to look at her, bobbed its head a few times and walked across her chest and down to her slightly raised knee. It ruffled its feathers a little, then took off. After swooping around the room once, it flew out the window.

"Now that's a friendly wake up call," said Denis as he climbed out of his hammock. He stretched and yawned.

Selamawit and Julia both mumbled as they got up, stretched and stared in amazement at Rohan. His legs, waist and chest were tied with blankets that held him to the hammock. He was still sleeping, but hanging underneath his hammock. He must have rolled over somehow in the night.

"I finally got tired of hearing him yelp every time he fell out," said Denis. "I guess I'd better untie him. Can one of you give me a hand, please?"

Selamawit moved over to Rohan's sleeping form and gave him a shake.

"Help! Ketiwe's got me in a full body lock!" Rohan tried to move his body and looked around in panic. "Why is everyone laughing?"

Denis and Selamawit gently untied Rohan and helped him to his feet.

"Thank you," he said.

"Wow! Morning breath!" cried Denis backing away.

"Sorry," said Rohan. He reached into his pocket and pulled out a small tube. "I have my travel toothbrush, does anyone have any toothpaste?"

Prunella laughed. "You remembered your toothbrush but not a flashlight. We really must work on our organization."

"I have a small amount of toothpaste left in my tube," said Selamawit quietly. "You may have some, Rohan."

"Thank you, Selamawit," said Rohan. "Now, I'm off to the bathroom."

Rohan walked to the door only to be met by a guard who raised his hand to halt the boy. The guard pointed to the floor, indicating that they all should sit.

"I suppose we have to wait for our hosts to decide when to kill us," said Prunella. "I hope they don't want us to play the game in the afternoon. Think of the heat."

Just then, three young Maya women entered the room. They were followed by two young men. The Strangers stood. Each of the women went to one of the girls, and the men to the boys. With smiles on their faces, they escorted the children out of the room and along a corridor.

"Any ideas, Denis?" asked Prunella.

Denis let out a breath and replied, "They're our personal slaves and are here to grant our every wish? Hey, where are you going?"

The girls were being led through a doorway, while the boys were taken further down the corridor, then through another door.

"This is near the bathroom," said Rohan. "It smells like water in here."

"Water doesn't have a smell," replied Denis, "but I know what you mean."

The two Maya led them into a small room. Here they

indicated that the boys should get undressed. Rohan and Denis quickly stripped down to their underwear.

"Mickey Mouse!" said Rohan.

"Not a word to anyone. Please, please," pleaded Denis. "They were a present from my older sister after she visited Disney World."

"She couldn't have brought you a t-shirt or a stuffed Donald?" said Rohan.

"My sister has a weird sense of humour," answered Denis. "Anyway, they're very comfortable," he added defensively.

Rohan simply smiled.

The Maya motioned the boys forward through another door. They entered a large room with a low partition down the middle. One side of the partition was a steam room. Where the boys had entered was a large pool. Rohan stepped forward a put a foot in the water.

"Cool! It's warm water. This is a giant bathtub." He stepped in all the way and sank down to his neck.

Denis followed quickly. "This feels good," he said and dunked his head under the water. "Is there any soap?"

"I didn't notice any. Just rub yourself down. It's mostly sweat anyway."

Denis moved to the edge of the pool and leaned against the side. "I wonder if the girls are getting the same kind of treatment. Ketiwe sure would appreciate this."

The two Maya moved towards the pool and grunted. They were each holding a large square of embroidered cloth.

"Looks like bath time is over," said Denis. He reached for one of the towels, but the Maya brushed his hand away and started to dry him. "They must think we're really special."

"My mum would kill me if I used a towel this nice to dry myself," said Rohan. "Everything here is so pretty and carefully made."

"They don't have factories and time cards. They can be more careful about what they do. And everything is some kind of homage to their gods." Denis finally took the towel and finished drying himself after he had slipped off his soaked Mickey Mouse shorts.

They went back into the other room and were shocked to find their clothes gone. In their place were two piles of brightly coloured Maya clothing.

Rohan picked up a long piece of cloth. "The sandals I can figure out, but what's this?"

One of the Maya came forward and took the cloth. Before Rohan knew what was happening, the man had wrapped the cloth around Rohan's waist, between his legs, and left the ends draped at the front and back. Denis received the same help. They were now wearing Maya breechclouts. They put on their sandals and then large square capes, like the one Ketiwe had been wearing.

"So, is this what the fashionable young Maya wears to the game of the week?" asked Rohan.

"It feels comfortable," answered Denis, " and looks good. But I hope we get our other clothes back. Those Nikes were expensive."

"And you wouldn't want to lose Mickey."

The Maya were waiting at the door, so the boys followed them. They were led back to their room and a few minutes later, the girls returned too. They were dressed in bright huipiles and skirts. Prunella's red hair hung loose down her back, but Julia and Selamawit had their long black hair tied back in braids, joined at the ends with ribbons.

"My, don't we look like Maya fashion plates," said Prunella.

"They were there to do our every bidding," said Selamawit. "They were so nice and the water was lovely. It was a shaded pool by the river. There were many fabulous birds in the trees."

"Did you lose your clothes, too?" asked Denis.

"Yes," replied Julia, "but I saw them all being put in a large basket by the door."

Bells ringing at the door made the children turn around. At the door stood five Maya soldiers, spears held at their sides. A man who was covered with a rainbow of feathers stood in the middle of them. He smiled and motioned towards the door.

"Show time," said Prunella as she moved forward.

The feathered man led the way and the soldiers followed behind the Strangers.

"Selamawit," said Rohan conversationally, "who's your favourite Disney character?"

Denis glared at him.

"Huey," she answered. "Tell me, Rohan, does Superman underwear not usually come with a cape?"

Julia screeched.

CHAPTER SEVENTEEN

The Strangers were led into the Palace courtyard. Here they were met by a large crowd of people, all of whom were wearing ceremonial garb. Everyone's clothing was adorned with bright feathers, very fine embroidery and pieces of jade, shell, painted wood, and obsidian. Canopies had been set up over many of the people to keep off the sun. As the canopies got larger and more fantastically decorated, the clothing of the people beneath became correspondingly more magnificent.

Chan-Bahlum sat cross-legged on a stone throne at the top of a short set of steps under the biggest canopy of all. The throne had two jaguar heads at its sides, both looking in at the King. Along the wall on either side of the steps were life-size reliefs of men. The two closest to the stairs were looking away, as if in fear of the King. All around on the walls were reliefs and carvings of flowers, birds, animals, and people. Glyphs were everywhere.

In awe, Denis said, "It must have taken them years to decorate this place."

Chan-Bahlum stood and the courtyard went silent. He spoke with a low, steady voice and everyone listened intently. Though the Strangers could not understand a word the King said, he held their attention. Such was the power of his voice. Several times he pointed at the children and smiled. He held a ball aloft and the crowd began to cheer. After a short while, the cheering died down and the King continued to speak. Finally, he grinned, said a few words and clapped his hands. Everyone sat down. Women began bringing trays and pots of food into the courtyard.

"Alright! Breakfast," said Rohan.

"More like lunch," said Julia as she looked skyward. "I

think we must have got up fairly late. The sun is almost overhead."

"There's Ketiwe's friend," whispered Prunella as a boy set down a pot of stew not far from them. He smiled at her when he saw that she was looking at him, then abruptly left the courtyard. "I wonder why he isn't waiting at the temple for her."

"He's probably being nonchalant, sizing up the situation for when Ketiwe gets back with Jozef. It's what people do when they're on a caper." Rohan said all this while stuffing juicy pieces of meat in his mouth.

"Do you ever leave time to breathe while you're eating?" asked Julia.

"Forgive my rudeness," said Rohan as he set down the corn cake he had just dipped in a green paste. "Sometimes when I'm hungry I forget my manners." He quickly retrieved the corn cake and took a huge bite after dipping it in some fish stew.

"You are always hungry, Rohan," said Selamawit. "This appetite of yours, it is not natural. Why can you not eat like a human child?"

"You'll end up weighing five hundred pounds," said Denis.

"And then you'll explode like that guy in the movie," added Prunella, "and there'll be guts all over the place."

"My uncle Gupta eats like this, and he is very thin like me. Big appetites run in my family. Could you please pass me some of that cocoa, Julia."

Prunella looked around the courtyard. The Maya were all busy eating and drinking. The women had joined in the feast now that the serving was completed.

"Have you noticed that the men seem to be getting drunk?" she asked.

Denis leaned forward. "I read that the Maya lords loved to

have banquets and they would get very drunk and have to be taken home by their wives. They drank some stuff called honeyfire."

The girls had looks of distaste on their faces. Rohan was busy chewing on a piece of meat.

Prunella shrugged and said, "It may work to our advantage when we try to make our escape."

The banquet continued for a few hours. The revellers were entertained by musicians playing an assortment of drums, rattles and horns. There were many dancers and at various times what appeared to be skits.

Soon many of the men in the courtyard were sleeping and the women began to clear away the remains of the food. Rohan made a quick grab for one last corn cake as the tray near him was removed.

"I wish we could get on with this," said Prunella. "All this waiting is making me nervous."

Just then the Chan-Bahlum entered the courtyard. He had left the revellers a short time before. He was now dressed even more colourfully. He had a high red headdress adorned with green feathers that shone in the sunlight. A long feathered robe fell from his shoulders to the ground. Beneath the robe, he wore a breechclout made from a jaguar pelt. From his neck hung many necklaces of jade and painted stones. Huge earrings made his earlobes hang almost to his shoulders.

The King clapped his hands and the sleepers began to rise. When everyone was standing, soldiers came to the Strangers and escorted them to the foot of the steps below the King. He smiled, turned and walked through the arch to the front of the Palace. The Strangers were formed into a line and marched after the King. As they emerged on the other side of the arch, they saw a line of five men waiting at the bottom of the stairs.

The men were large for Maya, one being almost six feet tall. They were dressed the same as the Strangers except that their hands were bound by rope. Behind the line stood more soldiers with spears aimed at the men's backs.

"I think we've just met the opposing team," said Denis, his voice a little shaky. "They're probably captives from a neighbouring city."

"They're full grown men. We have to play against adults. That's not fair!" cried Rohan.

"It doesn't matter that we're kids," answered Denis, "They think we've been sent by the gods. We can play against anyone."

The men in line looked up at the Strangers. They seemed puzzled by the sight of children who looked so different from everyone else. The big man didn't seem bothered at all. He simply began to grin and then started to laugh, not stopping until the soldier behind him smacked him on the head with the shaft of his spear.

"We are doomed," said Selamawit. "Do not try to convince me otherwise."

The Strangers descended the stairs to meet their opponents.

CHAPTER EIGHTEEN

The Strangers and the opposing team were lined up next to each other. Then, with the Chan-Bahlum at the head, a procession marched around the Palace, across the plaza, and up the steep steps of the Temple. At the top of the stairs waited two men who Denis speculated were priests. One held a large knife, the other a bowl.

"This could be gross," whispered Denis to Prunella who was just ahead of him.

The King marched straight up to the waiting priests. The two ball teams followed. The blazing sun made the climb a gruelling task. The King did not appear to be affected by the heat. When they reached the terrace just below the top, the teams were stopped. More people filed up the stairs and stopped at various terraces. When it seemed like every inch on the Temple's terraces was filled with people, the King turned to face the crowd below. The plaza was jammed with Maya, all straining to see what was happening at the top of the Temple.

The King was given the knife by one of the priests. The other priest held the bowl at the King's chin. The King said a few words, held the knife aloft, then stuck out his tongue and drove the knife through it. Blood spurted into the air and was caught in the bowl by the priest.

Rohan began to sway. "I think I'm going to throw up," he said. He was sweating profusely and all colour had drained from his face.

Selamawit grabbed him by the waist. "Hold on now, Rohan."

"Yeah," said Prunella. "We don't want the Maya to think you don't appreciate their cooking."

Rohan gave them a pained smile and swallowed hard. "I

think I'll be okay. Oh, no!"

As Rohan had been speaking, the King had pierced his left ear lobe. The priest caught the blood. Then the King pierced his right ear lobe.

"That is a terrible way to get pierced ears," said Selamawit. "Can you imagine if we had to do it ourselves at home?"

Rohan had closed his eyes and was holding a hand over his mouth.

"If you barf," said Julia, leaning close to Rohan, "then I'll barf too."

"And me," said Prunella.

"Likewise," added Denis.

"Imagine," said Selamawit, "everyone on the terraces throwing up together."

"Gross!" they shouted in unison.

The priests looked down at the Strangers and frowned. One had a particularly sour look on his face, as if he thought they had been making fun of him.

The King came forward and began to descend the steps. As he passed each terrace, the people on that terrace moved to the steps and followed him down. When they reached the plaza, the crowd parted. The people all stood in silence.

Prunella saw Chan again as they passed the front of the Palace. Soon they reached the ball court.

The Strangers were led to the end closest to the Palace, the captives to the other end. The King had made his way to the top of the "stands" and was seated on a stone bench. Ranged along the top of the court on both sides were dozens of nobles and their wives. Some of the men looked a little worse for wear; obviously, they had been at the banquet and had indulged themselves too much.

"Any ideas about how to play this game, Denis," asked

Prunella.

"Sure," he replied. "One member of the team stands forward, in the alley, while the rest stay back at the end, on the tee. Whoever is at the front has to try and get the ball through one of those hoops up on the sides."

"Easy," said Prunella. "We should be dead in about two minutes."

"Do not forget that you cannot use your hands or feet," said Selamawit.

"This is going to hurt a lot," said Julia.

"Hold on, it looks like we're going to get some padding," said Denis indicating the two men who were approaching them. Each man had a bundle of pads with him.

"Watch the other players and see what they do with the stuff," said Prunella. "We don't want to let on that we don't really know what we're doing here."

The Strangers gathered up the pads and looked down the court at the other team. Following their lead, they equipped themselves. Each of them put on a shin pad that came up past the knee and an arm pad that went from elbow to wrist. Over their chests and waists, they wore a thick belt of padding that tied up at the back.

"Do we have to wear these silly hats?" asked Rohan as he picked up what looked like an Apache headdress. He tried it on and it fit fairly well. Wood and jade ornaments hung down from the sides and rattled in his ears. The long red feathers stuck in the top curved back and almost touched the ground behind him.

"You look good, Rohan," said Selamawit, impressed by the young warrior beside her.

"Cool," replied Rohan.

"I wish we could wear pads on both shins and arms," said Prunella as she put on her headdress. It had a long jaguar tail in addition to all the feathers.

The other Strangers had put on all their equipment and stood examining each other. Most of their pads were red and white, while the other team was dressed in black and yellow.

"We're obviously the good guys," said Denis, "because we have the sort of white hats."

"I guess I'll go to the front first," said Prunella sheepishly. "After all, I am the captain."

"You can do it, Nell," shouted Julia as Prunella moved to the centre of the court.

A man from the other team moved to a position opposite Prunella. *At least he's not the huge guy*, she thought. *Thank you.*

The ball court was silent. The King stood, looked down at Prunella and her opponent, then threw the ball. It bounced between them. Instantly, the man was after the ball, elbowing Prunella out of the way. He chased the ball down the alley and, as it bounced off the side wall, swivelled his hips and sent the ball flying straight at Prunella. Unable to get out of its way, Prunella was hit right in the solar plexus by the hard sphere. The wind was knocked out of her and before she knew it, she was flat on her back.

The spectators broke into loud cheers. The man who had sent the ball crashing into Prunella ran by her, careful to plant a foot on her ankle as he passed, and retrieved the ball.

The pain in her ankle was tremendous. As she tried to stand, Prunella watched helplessly as the man used his elbow to send the ball hurtling towards one of the stone rings.

CHAPTER NINETEEN

Prunella sat on the ground at the end of the ball court. She winced as Julia massaged her ankle.

"Did I lose the game for us?" she asked.

"It doesn't look like it," answered Julia. "Denis is out there now, trying to score some points."

Denis was near the centre of the alley. He swung his hips and sent the rubber ball high into the air near where his friends were gathered.

"Gotta go," said Julia as she jumped up.

The ball bounced a few feet from where she stood. Julia sized it up then stooped and got her knee under it. The ball went sailing to the right, bounced near the foot of a spectator, and hit the ring. The crowd cheered, the Strangers groaned. It was so close.

Denis came panting back to the others.

"Your turn, Selamawit," he gasped. "Show 'em what you can do."

Selamawit leapt forward after the ball. In a flash she was at the other end of the court. She elbowed her opponent out of the way and chased the ball as it rolled down the alley. The other player ran after her, but Selamawit was the fastest girl on the Tyndale Junior High track team, and she wasn't about to let some man beat her to the ball.

She got to the ball, swooped down and used her forearm to scoop it up and onto the sloped wall. By the time the other player reached her, she had already hipped the ball into the air over his head and was running the other way. She ran straight at the low wall, bounced off it with one foot, and sprang into the air. Five feet over the alley floor she caught the ball with her shoulder and sent it flying through one of the rings.

The crowd went wild.

"Wow! Did you see that?" shouted Rohan.

The other Strangers, including Prunella, were jumping in the air cheering. Selamawit smiled bashfully and shrugged. Unfortunately, she was not paying attention to the other player. He came charging at her from behind and before she could heed the others' warning, he smashed into her and sent her skidding along the alley.

Selamawit landed on her elbow, the one not protected by a pad. The others ran to her and helped her up. A six inch scrape along her forearm was starting to bleed.

"It is not broken," Selamawit said calmly, "but my arm feels like it is burning. I think it hit my funny bone very hard. Rohan, could I borrow your handkerchief please?"

Rohan took out a blue hanky, he always carried at least two, and gave it to Selamawit. She gingerly wiped the blood from her arm then asked Rohan to tie the hanky around the place where the scrapes seemed the deepest.

"I am very sorry for soiling your handkerchief, Rohan. I will wash it out thoroughly when we get home."

"Don't worry about it," he said quietly, "I've got lots."

"Is that kind of thing legal in this game?" asked Julia.

"I don't know the rules, but I'd guess it's not entirely illegal." Denis turned to look at the other team. "They don't want to be sacrificed any more than we do."

"It's my turn now," said Rohan, his face a mask of anger.

Before anyone could stop him, Rohan had run to the middle of the alley. The King threw the ball out again and Rohan went for it. The other player was the same height as Rohan, but had at least sixty more pounds on him. He easily shoved Rohan out of the way and smacked the ball with his knee. Undeterred, Rohan charged after him. The Maya was running back from his end of the alley, right at Rohan. Rohan never slowed down. As he got closer to the Maya, he seemed to pick up speed. The Maya jumped up to use his chest on the ball. As he rose into the air, Rohan hit him just below the hips and flipped him over. The Maya landed on his back with a thud, the wind knocked out of him.

"That'll teach you to hurt my friend," he muttered.

Rohan ran to the end of the alley by the Strangers to get the ball. They stood there cheering him on, especially Selamawit, who was rubbing her wounded arm. Rohan swung his hips as the ball bounced off a spectator who was standing nearby and sent it back down the alley.

A new Maya player appeared and quickly sent the ball through the ring on the left. Rohan stopped in his tracks.

The King stood and waved his hands in the air. A man ran out onto the court and took the ball away. People began to leave the stands.

"Oh, no," cried Rohan. "I lost the game for us!"

CHAPTER TWENTY

"I'm so sorry. I tried." Tears poured down Rohan's face. "I didn't mean to get us sacrificed."

"It's okay," said Julia. "Look."

She pointed towards the Palace. Two young Maya were walking towards them carrying trays of fruit. At the other end of the ball court, the captive team was tucking in to their own trays of fruit.

Rohan's face instantly brightened. "Cool, just like back home when we played field hockey. At half time we would be given quartered oranges as refreshment."

As soon as the Maya with the food reached the Strangers, Rohan began to eat, all thoughts of being sacrificed forgotten.

Denis helped Prunella to her feet. Her ankle was still very sore, especially after jumping up and down after Selamawit had scored. She winced as she took a step and pushed Denis away when he tried to help her again.

"No, I've got to be able to move by myself if we're to make our escape." Prunella hobbled over to the Maya with the fruit.

Suddenly she pulled Denis and Julia close to her. "Those big feet," she said quietly, pointing at one of the servers. "That's Ketiwe."

"Why do you keep whispering?" asked Julia. "None of the Maya can understand what we're saying anyway."

"It's good practice in case we're ever anywhere where someone could understand us." Prunella took a piece of fruit. "Hello, Ketiwe, is Jozef with you?"

Ketiwe kept her head lowered so no one could see her speaking. "Yes. He's hiding in Chan's secret place until we can figure out how to get him into the game without attracting too much attention."

Rohan had heard the exchange between Prunella and

Ketiwe. He came over to them. "I know what to do. I'll get Chan to take me to the bathroom. While we're there, Jozef and I can switch clothes."

"But you don't look alike," Prunella protested. "The Maya will spot the difference in a second."

"So what?" replied Rohan. "We're supposed to be gods or something. We have powers. We can change what we look like anytime we want to. They'll just think we're mystical, magical..."

"Na-a-nee," sang Prunella. When the others just looked at her blankly, she added, "Nanny and the Professor. You guys really need to watch more of the magic box with me."

Ketiwe spoke up. "I could switch with you, Selamawit. You look hurt."

Selamawit shook her head in protest. "No. I am alright. It is only a small thing. I use my other arm to play the game."

As if to confirm that she was indeed alright, Selamawit swung her arms in the air and flexed her muscles. She only showed a little discomfort when she moved her hurt arm.

"Rohan's idea sounds like a good one," said Prunella. She wagged her finger at Rohan to indicate she wanted him to come closer. When he was right next to her, Prunella put her lips to his ear and whispered something. Rohan began to smile and nodded enthusiastically. "We're relying on you, Ro."

Rohan walked over to Chan and started to speak to him. After Rohan made a few gestures, Chan seemed to understand and ran to one of the guards standing nearby. They exchanged a few words and Chan looked back at Rohan and waved him over.

"Wish me luck," said Rohan happily, as he sprang off to join Chan.

The Strangers watched the pair walk off towards the

Palace, go up the front steps, and disappear through an doorway.

"It looks like I had better leave now," said Ketiwe.

The Maya serving the other team had appeared past the stands and were making their way back to the Palace. Ketiwe turned to go.

"Good luck," she said as she left.

CHAPTER TWENTY-ONE

"I'll go first this time," said Julia. She could see that Prunella was still favouring her hurt ankle, and Selamawit, though silent, was obviously in pain.

The Maya had returned to the stands. The King stood with the ball, waiting for the players to take their places. As Julia moved up, she could see that her opponent would be the huge Maya captive.

"Oh, no," she groaned, and looked back to her friends for encouragement. They all gave her the thumbs up sign and she turned to await the ball.

The ball bounced between the two players and took a wild hop to the right. Instead of going after the ball, the Maya grabbed Julia's wrist and gave a vicious twist. Before he knew what hit him, the Maya had been flipped over Julia's shoulder. He landed on the alley floor with a loud thump.

Julia looked down at him and grinned. "Judo, big boy," she said between clenched teeth. "Feel free to come back for more."

Julia dashed off after the ball. She hit it with her hips and the ball went straight at the ring up the right slope. Just like before, it hit just above the opening and bounced away.

Julia shouted, "POO!"

"NELL," came an insistent retort from the end of the alley. "NELL."

As Julia tried to stifle a giggle, the big Maya smacked the ball with his shin and scored a point. The crowd cheered and the big Maya gave Julia an arrogant look of triumph.

This time Julia took the initiative, and just before the ball bounced between her and the big Maya, she grabbed his chest pads and threw him to the ground. She raced after the ball but the Maya had recovered quickly and was right behind her before she could get the ball. Julia slowed slightly to let the Maya catch up, then swivelled and grabbed his arm. The Maya was soon flying through the air. He landed five feet up the left slope. The wind was knocked out of him.

Taking her time now that her opponent was out of the way for a few seconds, Julia sized up the situation. She took careful aim and hit the ball with her shin. It bounced off the left ring and down to the rest of the captive team.

Julia let out a blood curdling scream.

She stomped around in circles in the middle of the alley shouting, "Stupid, stupid game," over and over.

She only stopped when she heard Prunella call out, "Jozef's here."

Julia ran back to the end zone as Denis headed for the centre.

"Prunella's explaining how to play," he shouted as he passed Julia.

When Julia got close to Jozef and Prunella she stopped short and did a double take.

"Jozef! Why do you have that red stuff all over your face?" she asked, suppressing a grin.

"Ketiwe told me it would help me to blend in," he replied. "She said it washes off easily."

Prunella cut in, "Do you understand the rules, Jozef? No hands or feet."

He shook his head. "It's too bad I can't use my feet, but I've been practising my basket trick with my knees. We'll soon see how good it works."

Just then the crowd broke into loud cheering. The Strangers looked up to see Denis walking dejectedly from the alley. The other team had scored another point.

CHAPTER TWENTY-TWO

"The score's four to one for them," said Prunella.

"Show them all how it's done," said Denis as he slapped Jozef on the back.

"We know you can do it. You have great talent," said Selamawit.

Julia stood with her arms folded, a frown on her face. She stared straight down the alley at the other team. The big Maya looked right back at her, grinning. "Kick butt," was all she said.

Jozef walked to the centre of the alley. As he walked, the crowd became hushed. They must have noticed that he was different from the others. Though he and Rohan were both tall and slim, Jozef had long blond hair that the headdress couldn't hide. Except for Prunella, all the Strangers had dark hair and blended in easily with the black-haired Maya.

"Maybe they think you're an albino," shouted Julia. "It may make them even more wary of you."

The big Maya returned to the centre. He still looked arrogant. When he stopped in front of Jozef, he grunted and spat. The glob landed between Jozef's feet.

Jozef started to laugh. "Goo Goo G'Joob!" he cried as he lunged at the Maya. He waved his arms in the air.

The Maya was shocked by this and jumped back, his arrogance gone, replaced by confusion. The ball bounced at his feet but he hardly noticed.

Like lightning, Jozef moved forward and had the ball bouncing off his knees. As the Maya came at Jozef, a little wary of the crazy god in front of him, Jozef switched to his ankles and flipped the ball over the Maya's head. They ran around in circles for a few seconds. The ball never touched the ground. Jozef bounced it over the Maya's head, even off

the back of his head once. At last Jozef was in the position he wanted. He faked out the Maya, bounced the ball off the Maya's back, and kneed it through the left ring. While all this had been happening, Jozef had been singing Aerosmith's "Walk This Way."

The Strangers leapt for joy.

"Watch out for bad sports," shouted Prunella.

Jozef quickly turned around and was able to avoid the rushing Maya. A carefully placed foot sent the Maya sprawling to the ground.

"Two more like that," bellowed Denis.

Jozef waved and ran back to the centre to wait for the King to throw out the next ball. The big Maya did not look at all arrogant now, though it was obvious he was furious.

"That's good, big man," said Jozef slowly, "get mad and make mistakes."

This time the Maya was ready for the ball and ignored it. When he saw Jozef's eyes follow the path the ball had taken, the Maya just charged ahead and rammed a fist into Jozef's belly below his padding. Jozef's eyes popped out and he fell to his knees. As an added bonus, the Maya kneed the fallen boy in the side of the head.

Lucky for Jozef, the blow to his head landed on one of the wooden ornaments hanging from his headdress. He shook off the blow, recovered his breath, and chased after the Maya, singing something about being a beast of burden.

The Maya had just smacked the ball with his hip from the far end of the alley. The ball sailed low across the alley, steadily gaining height as it moved straight for the right ring.

Jozef ran as fast as he could and dove into the air. His arms were flung over his head and the padding on his right elbow just kissed the ball enough to send it bouncing down the slope. Jozef landed heavily on the slope and rolled down to the alley floor.

Breathing heavily, he got to his feet and muttered, "I suppose I could play goal for the team."

Play resumed. This time the Maya didn't try to hurt Jozef, but concentrated on the ball. He had it bouncing on his knees when Jozef ran into him. When Jozef moved away, the ball was now bouncing of his knees. While the Maya spun around looking for the ball, Jozef lined up another shot and scored a point.

The Strangers bounced around and cheered. They hugged each other. Julia and Prunella began to sing the Tyndale Junior High Victory Song, and Denis quickly joined in. Only Selamawit remained silent as she looked away and rubbed her head.

As Jozef returned to the centre of the alley, he could hear his fellow Strangers behind him.

"Only one more and we're tied!"

"You can do it, Jozef!"

"Wigrac!" That was Selamawit practising her Polish. She even had the pronunciation correct, saying it like "vi-grach."

A new Maya joined Jozef at the centre. The big man seemed to have had enough for a while. Jozef could see him kneeling in the other end zone. He was rubbing his thigh and talking to his teammates.

There are many fouls the officials do not see, he thought.

The new Maya was faster than his big teammate, but he was not the star of the Tyndale Falcons. Try as he might, the Maya could not retain control of the ball. Jozef missed several attempts at scoring points; he needed more practice to perfect his trick. Still, the other team did not score any points either.

Jozef had been running around the ball court for fifteen minutes now, and the heat was beginning to take its toll. He was sweating profusely and the pads were itching intensely. He could barely gasp out the words to "You Could Be Mine" by Guns 'n' Roses.

The Maya made a shot at the right ring. The ball bounced off the back wall, hit the inside of the ring, spun, and fell out. No point was scored. As the ball rolled off the slope, Jozef caught it with his knees and sent it into the air. The Maya intercepted the ball with his shoulder and sent it careening off the left wall. Jozef leapt into the air and gave the ball a good butt with his head.

Score!

The game was tied!

Jozef ran slowly over to his friends. "I need a rest," he gasped. "Someone else must play for a while."

"I'll do it," said Denis, and he ran off to the centre.

"If Denis can keep the other team from scoring until you're ready to play again," said Prunella, "we can win this game."

"But we must not win the game!" cried Selamawit.

"What do you mean?" asked Julia. "That's the whole point, isn't it?"

"We must not win the game," repeated Selamawit. "The captain of the losing team will be sacrificed."

"I don't want to be sacrificed," said Prunella impatiently.

"We cannot allow the captain of the other team to die. It would not be right," shouted Selamawit.

"But he probably would be killed anyway," said Jozef. "He's a captive. That's what happens to captives."

"That may be true," said Selamawit, "but we are playing this game because we are here. If we had not come out from the Temple, these men might not have been playing this game. If their captain dies, it will be our fault."

The others had fallen silent.

"We must not be responsible for the death of another person. It is not right."

CHAPTER TWENTY-THREE

"Julia!" shouted Prunella. Julia turned to face her. "You take a turn in the alley, I need to talk to Denis. I've got to think."

Before Julia could leave, Selamawit grabbed her arm.

"Let me go please," said Selamawit softly, "I want another chance at the game."

Selamawit ran off to the alley. She exchanged a high five with Denis as he left. The big Maya had returned to play. Selamawit stood in front of him and looked up into his face. She was very small next to the man. He started to laugh and Selamawit slapped his face. The man was startled but unhurt. He rubbed his cheek and stared down at the girl. She stood defiantly.

"Please laugh again," she said.

As if he understood her, the Maya smiled and nodded his head. Her bold act had impressed the man. Selamawit gave her opponent a salute.

The ball bounced between them and they ran off after it.

"Denis," said Prunella as the Strangers stood watching Selamawit keep the ball away from her opponent, "if they're going to sacrifice the loser, where will they do it?"

Denis thought for a moment. "Most likely it will be at the Temple. That's where the old king is buried. I'd guess it's the most sacred place in Palenque right now. We first appeared there, and this game seems to be in honour of us and Pacal."

"Good," said Prunella. Her brows furrowed and she paced around the end zone. After a few seconds, she said, "I've got Rohan working on something that should help us to escape. If everything goes right, we shouldn't have any problem getting away."

"What is it?" asked Jozef.

"I want it to be a surprise, for everyone," was all that Prunella would say.

Prunella walked closer to the alley and shouted to Selamawit. "It's okay, Sela, you can let him have the ball now. We want the other team to win."

Selamawit reacted immediately. She kneed the ball into the Maya's face then ran back to the end zone.

"Jozef," she said breathlessly, "I believe you would be the best among us at pretending to try to win."

"No problem." Jozef ran back to the centre, singing, "We aren't the champions, my friend," as the Maya scored a point.

For another ten minutes, Jozef made a valiant effort to score points. Almost every time he got the ball, he was able to feed it to his opponent while making it look like it had been stolen. He took a couple of inaccurate shots at the rings. Twice he managed to bounce the ball off spectators who were not paying attention to the game.

Suddenly the spectators went quiet. The King stood and raised his arms to the sky. The captive team began to cheer and clap each other on the back. The game was over.

Guards ran out from behind the stands and surrounded the Strangers. They herded the children into a line, with Prunella at the front, then stood at attention. The other team came up beside them. The big Maya was at the head of the line and turned to look at Prunella. He smiled and shook his head in approval. Prunella smiled back and saluted him.

A couple of young Maya boys ran up and began to remove the protective padding the players were wearing. One of the boys was Chan. He gave Prunella a thumbs up when he saw her glance at him. When all the padding was off the players, the boys ran off.

The King, followed by his entourage, moved across the plaza to the Palace. The guards indicated with their spears that the teams should follow. They crossed the plaza amidst cheering Maya. The regular folk of the city had been crowded at either end of the ball court straining to see the action. Some had gathered on the terraces of the temple across the plaza from the Palace. This had afforded them a good view of the game.

"Why are they so happy that their enemies won the game?" asked Selamawit.

"It's all ceremonial," replied Julia. "Winning doesn't really matter. I think we've just finished acting out a battle between the Maya's gods. They don't care who wins because none of them are going to be sacrificed."

"That makes me feel so much better," said Prunella sarcastically.

They reached the bottom of the Palace steps and halted. The King was seated on his jaguar throne, a stern look on his face. A priest came down the steps and stood before the captive captain. He placed a necklace of jade around the man's neck. Maya girls came from the side of the Palace and presented each of the winning players with a pot. From the strong smell emanating from the pots, Prunella guessed they had just received the Maya equivalent of victory champagne.

The winners looked up at the King. His face had relaxed a bit. He waved his hand at the winners and pointed away to the north. The winners looked surprised for a moment, then turned and ran off in the direction of the northern plains.

"He's just set them free," said Denis. "I think they were expecting to be made slaves."

The priest turned his attention to Prunella.

"Uh oh," she said.

The priest reached into his robe and took out a length of rope. Guards grabbed Prunella's arms and thrust them forward. The priest quickly tied the girl's wrists together.

Prunella winced. "Hey, not so tight, you beast." She tried to kick the man. He scuttled out of her way.

"Hah! Still nervous about touching the red-haired goddess, eh?" Prunella took a step towards the priest. He made a choking noise and retreated to a spot behind the King.

Prunella looked around where she stood.

"Any of you guys see Rohan or Ketiwe?" she asked the others.

The Strangers looked around but no one said yes.

"Okay Rohan," she shouted, "we're waiting."

Nothing happened.

"I said, WE'RE WAITING!"

Silence.

The King stood and the guards converged on the Strangers.

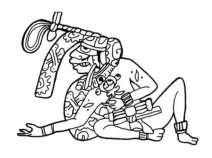

CHAPTER TWENTY-FOUR

The Strangers walked slowly across the plaza. As they came around the side of the Palace, they could see the Temple of Inscriptions. Many of its terraces were already filled with people, all standing silently, waiting for their King.

"What's supposed to be happening, Nell?" asked Denis.

Without turning her head, Prunella answered, "Rohan is supposed to help us escape by causing a distraction. He must have been captured."

Prunella looked all around her. To her left was the only tower in Palenque, a part of the Palace. As she took in its height, she thought she saw someone on the top level. She tried to see into the shadow there, but...

"ROCK AND ROLL!"

Everyone stopped. The words had come from the right of the Strangers, but they could see nothing but a sea of Maya.

Crack! Crack! Crack! Crack! Boom!

Someone screamed. The explosions had come from next to the Palace. Many of the Maya fell to the ground, their heads covered by their hands.

"That's Rohan," shouted Prunella, "run for the temple."

"Better not," someone shouted, "a whole bunch of Maya are running that way."

Crack! Crack! Boom!

"Run through the Palace! Ketiwe's just inside."

As they ran up the steps, Prunella realized the voice was Rohan, shouting down from the tower. So she had seen someone up there.

The Strangers ran into the Palace and were met by Ketiwe who said nothing but beckoned them to follow. Running at full tilt, the children soon made it to the far side of the Palace. Behind them they could hear an occasional crack! and boom!

and the odd scream.

They encountered no one as they left the Palace. They jumped down some steps and ran through the arch under the aqueduct near the kitchen. Soon they were running through a cornfield. Ketiwe slowed to a walk and waved the others to silence. In a few moments, they emerged next to the aqueduct at Chan's secret place. There was plenty of room for the six of them to fit inside.

"Do we have to do any more running? I'm out of breath." Prunella leaned back against the alcove wall. "And could someone please untie my hands?" Denis stepped forward.

"Speak quietly," said Ketiwe. "Though the path is a fair distance from here, we don't want to take any chances. The Maya might be looking for us."

"You don't think they'll believe we've gone back into the tomb or to wherever it is their gods live?" asked Prunella.

"One of them may have seen us run through the Palace. We should always be careful," said Selamawit. She rubbed her arm where the hanky covered the scratches. Sweat was making the cuts sting a little.

Jozef walked to the edge of the alcove and looked out. "Where's Rohan?"

"I saw him up in the tower," said Prunella. "Does he know how to get here, Ketiwe?"

"Chan and I brought him straight here after he switched places with Jozef. That basket in the corner has all your clothes in it. Rohan had no problem finding the matches and firecrackers."

"What firecrackers?" asked Julia.

Prunella grinned. "I had some left from the holiday, along with the matches. I was saving them for the boys' locker room at school."

"I hope Rohan is able to find his way back here. We

cannot leave without him. I still have his handkerchief. I must return it to him."

"Don't worry, Sela," said Ketiwe, "Rohan knows his way about."

As she said this, there was a rustling in the corn. They all went silent and froze. The noises got closer to the alcove and they could see the tops of corn stalks moving a few rows away. Ketiwe picked up a piece of stone that was lying near her foot. Denis and Jozef had their fists ready.

Two huge birds waddled into view. They had bald blue heads with large yellow bulges between their eyes. Their bodies were copper coloured and their tail feathers were very long.

"They look like a cross between a turkey and a peacock," said Julia.

"Go away dumb birds," said Ketiwe, "I'm tired of being stalked by animals."

The birds ignored her and continued to peck at the ground. Soon they moved on.

"How long do we have to stay here?" asked Jozef.

Ketiwe, who had sat down again, drew a sun then a moon in the dust. Then she said, "It's best if we wait until dark. It shouldn't be much longer."

"It looks like it's going to rain again," Julia observed. "And sounds like it, too," she added as thunder rumbled somewhere off in the distance.

Within minutes it was impossible to see out of the alcove, the rain was so heavy. Ketiwe eased herself as far back into the alcove as she could to avoid the splattering rain. The sky was soon black and the rain seemed to get even heavier. Despite the heat of the day, there was a distinct chill in the air. The Strangers huddled together for warmth.

As they sat, a figure passed through the curtain of rain at

the alcove's entrance. A sodden Rohan materialized there, a gooey mess in his right hand.

"I think my corn cake got wet," was all he said.

CHAPTER TWENTY-FIVE

It had stopped raining hours ago. Julia stood at the edge of the alcove watching the sky. Ketiwe had shown her the diagram that Chan had scratched into the wall.

"It's the constellation Pegasus," said Julia as soon as she saw it.

"Chan drew this and a moon then pointed to the sky," explained Ketiwe.

Julia thought for a moment then said, "We have to wait here until we can see Pegasus in the sky."

Now she stood waiting for the constellation to appear above the corn. The other Strangers sat and fidgeted. Sitting silently in the cramped space for so long had been extremely uncomfortable.

Rohan had wanted to change into his regular clothes after his soaking in the rain. Prunella had suggested they keep their Maya stuff on in case someone saw them as they tried to reach the Temple.

"From a distance, we'll look like a bunch of Maya kids out for some fun," she had said. "I wonder if Maya kids go out at night and look for fun."

"There it is," said Julia. "Let's roll."

They got up and stretched, yawned and rubbed the cramps from their muscles. Prunella tested her ankle and, despite the ugly bruise, was able to walk on it with little discomfort. Rohan had produced yet another hanky and used rainwater to clean Selamawit's arm. The bleeding had stopped, and now it only throbbed.

"Let me lead," whispered Ketiwe, "I've been this way before."

Quietly they left the alcove in a single file. Rohan went last and carried the basket with their clothes. They moved into the corn a few rows, then headed right towards the path. When they reached the edge of the corn next to the path, Ketiwe halted them and went to step out.

"Rock and roll," someone whispered from the shadows.

The gang froze as a shape separated from the shadows and crossed the path. Soon they were joined in the corn by Chan.

He gave them a thumbs up and repeated, "Rock and roll."

"I had to teach him something to say to distract the Maya in the plaza," said Rohan. " Rock and roll sounds so cool when it's yelled out."

Chan cautioned them to be quiet and motioned them to the ground. They dropped and lay as flat as possible between the rows of corn and waited as some men approached. The men came through the arch under the aqueduct and went down the path to the small bridge. Soon they crossed the river and were out of sight on the other side.

Chan got up and led the Strangers out of the corn. Rather than go through the arch, as Ketiwe had expected, they crossed the path and followed the aqueduct. This kept them in the shadows. Light from the full moon would have made anyone in the open a sitting duck. Another cornfield kept them hidden from the river.

Soon they came to the point where the aqueduct met the river. Chan waited a moment then waded into the water. The Strangers hesitated and Chan looked back at them impatiently. They could tell he wanted them to "get a move on."

Despite her obvious reluctance, Ketiwe was the first one to follow Chan into the water. As she neared him, he took her hand and held on tight.

Ketiwe looked back to the others. "Pair up," she whispered, "The current is fast and the bottom is slippery."

Denis and Prunella slipped into the river and almost

immediately Prunella tripped on a slimy stone and went under. Denis kept a tight grip on her hand and pulled her up right away. She spat out some water and brushed her hair from her face. Denis tried not to laugh as he removed a large leaf that was stuck to the back of her head.

Julia and Jozef were next, followed by Rohan and Selamawit. Rohan had the basket of clothes balanced on his shoulder. Selamawit held on to his arm with both hands. She would make absolutely sure he didn't fall.

The water was about three feet deep and once the children were used to the current and the slippery river bed, they had no trouble moving along. They had all crouched down so only their heads and Rohan's shoulder were above water. This way they might be mistaken for a flock of birds.

A couple of times as they made their way along the river, they had to stop as Maya walked by on the path above them. Reeds along the bank kept the Strangers out of sight, but also gave them a few frights. Twice, large animals rushed from the reeds and up the riverbank. Something long swam past Julia but she stayed quiet and watched it move away.

Eventually they came to the place on the river near the small temple where Ketiwe had first met Chan. They waited in the water beside a couple of canoes while Chan ran up to the temple to check things out. Soon he signalled that they could move up.

When they were all standing behind the temple, Rohan started to take clothes out of the basket. Chan stopped him and pointed into the forest.

"I'm going to get all muddy again," said Ketiwe flatly. "I am not amused."

"There's a nice hot shower waiting for you at Strange House," Prunella said and sneezed.

Denis looked up into the forest where Chan was waiting.

"We'd better get moving."

The forest had been dark when Ketiwe had first entered it yesterday afternoon. Now it was pitch black. Chan took Ketiwe's hand again. Ketiwe grabbed Prunella's and a chain was quickly formed. There were no mishaps and in no time they were standing at the edge of the forest behind the Temple of Inscriptions.

Chan motioned for them to sit and remain quiet. He stepped out of the forest and onto a terrace. He crawled along on his hands and knees and disappeared around a corner. The Strangers waited in tense silence. When Chan reappeared, they began to move forward but he quickly stopped them.

Chan did not look happy. With the Strangers gathered round him, he signed to Ketiwe what he had found. He counted off five fingers then made a stabbing motion with both hands, as if using a spear.

"Five guards," she said.

Chan counted off two more fingers and hesitated.

"Two others, but he doesn't seem to know how to tell us who they are."

"It doesn't matter," said Prunella. "How can seven kids go up against five grown men with spears. It looks like we're stuck here after all.

CHAPTER TWENTY-SIX

"It worked before, it can work again," said Rohan, clearly excited. He was fumbling through the basket of clothes. Shortly he exclaimed, "Aha!" and pulled out a string of firecrackers.

"I didn't want to take them all for our escape," he said. "You know, just in case. My caution paid off."

The Strangers started to cheer but quickly hushed when they remembered the soldiers on the other side of the Temple.

"Good old Rohan, always prepared," whispered Julia.

"I used to be a Boy Scout," he answered, "but I quit because I don't like selling apples."

"They're not nearly as good as Girl Guide cookies," agreed Prunella.

"I prefer those chocolate covered almonds we sold last year at school," said Ketiwe. "I like to plop one in my mouth then chew off all the chocolate until just the nut is left."

Denis tapped Ketiwe on the shoulder. "No, no. Have you ever tried to crack a Smartie in half and lick the chocolate out of the centre without breaking the shell?"

"That's easy," scoffed Julia. "Try biting the back off a Caramilk square then licking out the caramel without breaking the chocolate cup. That takes talent."

"Excuse me, please," Selamawit cut in, "but should we not be planning our escape? We can discuss the best way to eat candy when we get home."

The other Strangers looked at Selamawit as if she had just interrupted an extremely important debate. She stood there, staring at them, waiting for someone to say something. Finally, Prunella spoke up.

"Rohan, do you have any matches left?"

"Sure," he answered, and reached into the cloth tied around his waist. He pulled out a matchbox and slid it open. Water and soaked matches fell out the bottom and scattered on the forest floor. Rohan looked horrified. The others groaned.

"Wait!" Denis cried, then ducked his head in terror. "Sorry," he said quietly.

The others came out from behind the trees where they had sought cover at Denis' outburst. They looked towards the Temple but nothing had seemed to change.

"What?" said Prunella impatiently.

"My mother collects matchbook covers. Gerry Dawson's older brother gave him a matchbook from that new restaurant where he works. Gerry gave me the matchbook just before the soccer game yesterday. It should still be in my shirt pocket."

Denis went to the basket of clothes and fumbled through it. He took out his shirt and fished out the matchbook. When the others were distracted by a noise in the forest, he shoved a small bundle of cloth with a mouse on it into his breechclout.

"Nuts," he said in disgust, "they've all been set off. Gerry's brother must have not wanted to take any chances with little kids getting hold of the matches and burning down the school again."

Chan had been watching all that had passed. He came up to Rohan and took the string of firecrackers. "Boom?" he asked. Rohan nodded. Chan gave them the thumbs up and beckoned them to follow. He moved to a spot at about the centre of the back of the Temple and stepped out onto the terrace. The others followed. They didn't need to be told to stay quiet.

Chan quickly clambered up to the next terrace. Here he

lay down and reached a hand down to whomever was going to climb up next. Denis and Rohan stood facing each other and formed a step with their linked hands. In no time, the others were all on the next terrace.

They repeated this two more times until they were on the terrace right below the main structure of the Temple. They crawled along the terrace towards the left side of the Temple, facing away from the Palace. As they reached the corner, they could see several smaller temples below, but no one could be seen around them. The Temple of Inscriptions seemed to be the only building important enough to warrant guards for the night.

Moving at a snail's pace, they crawled towards the front of the Temple. When Chan reached the front corner, he put his hand up to stop the others. Ketiwe, who was next in line behind Chan, moved up next to him and looked around the corner.

The five guards each stood in front of one of the entrances to the Temple. One of them was almost directly above where Ketiwe crouched. She shrank back into the shadows a little. At the bottom of a short flight of stairs leading to the terrace on which the Strangers were gathered, two priests seemed to be performing some kind of ritual. Torches were burning in two rows down the entire length of the staircase to the plaza. As the breeze blew on the flames, eerie shadows moved all over the front of the Temple. Down below, the plaza was deserted.

Chan slipped a hand under his cape and brought out a small pouch. He opened the pouch and took out a book bound with jaguar skin and what looked like a quill pen. These he presented to Ketiwe. She looked shocked but took the gifts. Chan smiled at her then made a move to go back along the terrace. Ketiwe grabbed his arm, pulled him close, and gave him a quick kiss on the cheek. This flustered the boy for a moment, but he quickly gathered his wits and moved off. He seemed to move with more of a spring in his step.

The Strangers remained where they lay and watched Chan climb up to the side of the Temple building. Slowly he was able to make it up onto the roof. There was a narrow lip all around the roof. He followed this lip to the back of the building where he began to climb even higher. A roof comb rose almost forty feet towards the sky. Covered with reliefs and carvings, it resembled a giant billboard at the top of the Temple. Chan moved with great care and took his time so as not to make any noise that could alert the guards and priests below.

When he reached a spot near the centre, he braced himself and looked out over the plaza. He was over a hundred feet up and the view made him a little dizzy. He nestled into the jaws of a huge serpent to brace himself.

Boom!

A torch burning next to one of the priests exploded. The guards moved to the edge of the top terrace to get a better look. The priest next to the exploded torch was flat on his back, a look of sheer terror on his face.

Crack! Crack! Crack!

Three torches near the guards exploded sending showers of sparks everywhere. The guards screamed and four ran for the centre staircase. The priests were already half way down the stairs. The remaining guard didn't bother with the stairs and simply jumped down to the next terrace.

Boom! Crack! Boom!

Torches continued to explode and the guards moved even faster. The gods must be really angry at someone.

Once the guards were a couple of terraces down, the Strangers scrambled into action. They got up and ran as fast

as they could for the front steps. They bounded up the short flight to the main entrance and ran in. Ketiwe looked up in time to see Chan edging his way along the roof comb. She didn't think anyone would see him from the plaza.

"Thank you, Chan," she shouted. "You take care of yourself."

Denis grabbed one of the unexploded torches as he entered the Temple and took the lead. He stopped when he reached the entrance to the passage down to the tomb. Everyone was here except Prunella.

"Hurry up, Nell, we haven't got all night," he shouted.

Prunella had stopped just as she was about to enter the Temple. Something made her turn and look down at the Palace. There, near where the Strangers had made their escape that afternoon, stood Chan-Bahlum. He was looking straight at Prunella. She looked back and waved. Above the screams of the retreating guards and priests, Prunella was sure she could hear a deep bellowing laugh. Chan-Bahlum waved back.

Prunella rushed in to join the others. Quickly they descended the steps, Denis in the lead with the torch. When they reached the landing where the stairs turned, Denis halted them.

"Jozef and Rohan," he said quickly, "give me your capes. Wait here until I call you."

With that, Denis went down to the tomb entrance.

"Okay," he shouted up after a moment, " come on down."

As they went down, Selamawit began to cough. "What is that horrible smell?"

Julia answered from behind her, "It's those people who were sacrificed the other day. They don't keep well in this heat. Try to ignore the stench."

"I cannot ignore it. It is like some giant slug trying to

crawl up my nose and into my head."

"I've seen that movie," said Rohan.

At the bottom of the stairs, Denis stood waiting. Behind him the bodies were covered with the capes. The stone slab was still to one side.

"At least they didn't reseal the tomb," he said. "We would have been in real trouble then. They must have been nervous about coming back down here after our appearance."

"Enough of this talk!" shouted Selamawit, clearly uncomfortable. "I do not wish to be ill!"

They moved into the tomb. The torches had burned out, and there were crawling things in the shadows. They crossed to where the door to the tunnel should have been. Prunella began to press various knobs and carvings. Ketiwe came forward.

"Let me," she said and stuck her finger in the eye of a toad. "I spent two hours here yesterday trying to find the way out."

The door swung open and the Strangers passed through. When they were all in the tunnel, Jozef pushed the door shut.

"I think we're safe now," said Prunella, " except for Uncle Archie."

CHAPTER TWENTY-SEVEN

The Strangers were flopped in various places around Prunella's room in Strange House. Prunella had directed each of them to one of the seemingly endless number of bathrooms in the mansion. They had showered and changed back into their regular clothes.

Denis had felt bad about not bringing back the ball that had originally been in the Mayan room.

"Don't worry," said Prunella, "Uncle Archie will never notice. There's so much stuff in this house, he can't possibly remember everything. Anyway, all those genuine Maya clothes should more than make up for it."

Jozef still had a wash cloth and kept trying to rub off the red goo that had been painted on his face. Every now and then he glared over at Ketiwe. She seemed to be oblivious to Jozef's gaze, intent only on examining the book Chan had given her.

Denis looked up from the book he was reading. He was tucked in a big armchair in one corner.

"This is interesting," he said. "The Maya wrote thousands of books. Most of them were burned by the Spanish after the Conquest. Chan could have been training to be a scribe."

"That small temple where we came out of the river was some kind of library," said Ketiwe. "Chan showed it to me when we first met. Maybe he worked there."

"That book he gave you could be some kind of letter."

Ketiwe looked at the scroll for the hundredth time. "Can you tell me what it says?"

Denis held up the book he was reading. "This has some Mayan words translated, but it'll be a lot of work to figure out what Chan had to say to you."

"You will probably want to translate it by yourself," said

Selamawit. "I think Chan liked you, and the message may be personal."

Rohan bristled at hearing this. He was seated on the floor next to Denis' chair, and when he moved to say something, Denis grabbed his shoulder.

"I told you to give it up, Ro. She'll kill you."

"After facing death a thousand years ago, I'm going to be afraid of a girl?" Rohan laughed.

There was a knock at the door, and Mohan Singh walked in. He was carrying a tray with a teapot and several cups on it. A plate of his special oatmeal chocolate chip cookies sat next to the pot.

"I thought you all might like some refreshments after your adventure," he said solemnly.

He set the tray down on a table near the bottom of the bed. Before he could finish pouring the first cup, Rohan had a mouth full of cookie. He was soon joined by Jozef who had developed a passion for Mohan Singh's cookies.

When he had finished pouring the tea, Mohan Singh turned to Selamawit. He took a pouch and a small bottle out of one of the big pockets of his safari jacket.

"Miss Selamawit, I think I should dress that wound on your arm. We would not want it to get infected. Your mother might not allow you to return to Strange House, and that would be very sad."

Selamawit seemed a little embarrassed at this attention, but submitted herself to Mohan Singh's care. Soon he was finished and turned to leave. As he passed Denis, Mohan Singh dropped a small paper bag in his lap. There was a sharp intake of breath when Denis looked in and saw Mickey Mouse looking back at him.

"Your sister would be most unhappy if she learned you had lost her most valuable present, young sir," said Mohan Singh.

Denis quickly stuffed the bag into his back pocket and checked around to see if anyone had seen what had just happened.

At the door, Mohan Singh turned and said, "You might want to look at the drawing on the back wall of the Maya room. It depicts one of the temples at Palenque as it looked when Mr. Catherwood did his wonderful work back in the nineteenth century, before the face of the temple had been completely eroded by the weather."

"I will return shortly with more cookies." He closed the door.

Rohan had just stuffed another cookie in his mouth and Julia was looking miffed because she had only been able to get half of one of Ketiwe's cookies.

"How do you suppose he knew where we'd been?" asked Jozef.

As if to answer the question, a whistled "Do Wah Diddy" could be heard receding down the hallway.

The Strangers made their way back to the Maya room and straight to the drawing on the back wall. It was a magnificent work of art with intricate detail that showed every carving and relief.

"Wow!" said Denis. "I didn't see this before."

They all looked closer as he pointed out a series of reliefs above the entrances to a temple. Six figures were there, clear as day. They represented players of the ball game. Five of them were obviously not Maya.

The first was Prunella with her long hair flying around her head like the corona around the sun. Then came Julia, her left foot resting on the back of an opponent whom she had just flipped over her shoulder. Denis was holding a ball, ready to play. Selamawit's fine Ethiopian features were unmistakeable. She was running like the wind. Rohan was bouncing a ball on

his knee, but where the real Rohan had short hair, this one had Jozef's long flowing locks.

The last figure was the most unusual. He was a young Maya. His arms were raised over his head and one hand held an open book, the other a brush. Little starbursts were all around him.

"Chan-Bahlum must have figured out what Chan did to help us," said Denis. "It looks like he didn't get into any trouble for it."

"Neat," was all Rohan could say.

They heard someone pass outside the door, and the aroma of freshly baked oatmeal and chocolate chip cookies wafted in. The Strangers turned to go.

"Maybe Mohan Singh put raisins in this batch," said Rohan. "That makes them juicier."

"You're so gross, Ro," replied Julia. "Raisins look like dead fly bodies, and don't taste much better."

Rohan stared at Julia with his mouth hanging open. "You've tasted dead flies? Neat!"

GLOSSARY

Catherwood, Frederick - An artist who did very detailed drawings of Maya ruins during the 1830s and 1840s.

Chac - The Mayan word for east or red. This symbolized the sunrise.

Chan-Bahlum - Pronounced Can-Bah-LOOM. He was the son of Pacal (Shield). He came to the throne in 683 A.D. when Pacal died. His succession ceremonies would have taken place some time in January 684. His name means Serpent Jaguar. He may have had acromegaly.

Chiki - The Mayan word for west or black. This symbolized sunset.

Palenque - From the Spanish word for palisade. It is located in the northern part of the Mexican state of Chiapas.

Pok-to-Pok - Pronounced Pahk-toh-pahk. The ball game.

Tupil - Pronounced too-peel. The Mayan word for policeman.

Xibalba - Pronounced Sheebalba. The Maya underworld. The nine terraces of the Temple of Inscriptions represent the nine underworlds.

BIBLIOGRAPHY

Brosnahan, Tom. La Ruta Maya. Lonely Planet Publications Inc., Berkeley, 1991.

Canby, Peter. The Heart of the Sky: Travels Among the Maya. Harper Collins, 1992

Gorenstein, Shirley. Not Forever On Earth. Charles Scribners Sons, New York, 1975

Hunter, C. Bruce. A Guide to Ancient Maya Ruins. University of Oklahoma Press, Norman, 1974.

Karen, Ruth. Song of the Quail: The Wondrous World of the Maya. Four Winds Press, New York, 1972.

Morris, Walter F., Jr.. Living Maya. Harry N. Abrams, 1987.

Sabloff, Jeremy A.. The Cities of Ancient Mexico: Reconstructing A Lost World. Thames and Hudson, New York, 1989.

Schele, Linda and David Friedel. A Forrest of Kings: The Untold Story of the Ancient Maya. William Morrow and Co., New York, 1990.

Stuart, George E. and Gene S. Stuart. The Mysterious Maya. National Geographic Society, Washington, D.C., 1977.